NINE-TO-FIVE
BRIDE

NINE-TO-FIVE BRIDE

BY

JENNIE ADAMS

™MILLS & BOON®

First published in Great Britain 2009
Large Print edition 2009
Harlequin Mills & Boon Limited,
Eton House, 18-24 Paradise Road,
Richmond, Surrey TW9 1SR

© Jennifer Ann Ryan 2009

ISBN: 978 0 263 20617 3

Set in Times Roman 16½ on 18¼ pt.
16-0809-53431

Harlequin Mills & Boon policy is to use papers that are
natural, renewable and recyclable products and made
from wood grown in sustainable forests. The logging and
manufacturing process conform to the legal environmental
regulations of the country of origin.

Printed and bound in Great Britain
by CPI Antony Rowe, Chippenham, Wiltshire

For Fiona Harper and Melissa McClone.
How much fun was this?

For Joanne Carr and Kimberley Young, with thanks for
making the www.blinddatebrides.com trilogy a reality.

And to the special man in my life—I won't tell
we agreed on marriage on our first date if you don't!

CHAPTER ONE

'YOU want us to turn this smaller bridge into a clone of the historic Pyrmont Bridge. I'm sorry, but we can't do that for you. The sites simply don't compare.' The boss of the Sydney-based Morgan Construction, Building and Architecture braced his feet on the uninspiring bridge in question, drew a deep breath and blew it out as he addressed the middle-aged man at his side.

Rick Morgan's rich voice held an edge of command and control that shivered over Marissa Warren's senses. The three of them stood atop the small Sydney bridge while the Morgan's boss explained the company's stance on the refurbishment plans. Rick could bring about virtually any architectural feat, be it in refurbishment or new construction. What he wasn't prepared to do was break his own code of working standards.

A pity Marissa couldn't push away her equally unfeasible reactions to the man. She hadn't expected an attack of awareness of the company's big boss. The girls in the office swooned about Rick, but Marissa was no longer interested in hot corporate types. Been there, so over that.

It must be the sway factor of the bridge getting to her. Or the sea wind pressing hard against her back trying to disrupt her balance. Those must be responsible for the odd feelings coursing through her.

Anything other than genuine attraction to this corporate high-flyer who owned the large company that employed her. Since she'd started at Morgan's six months ago she hadn't said more than 'good morning' to the boss in passing and, frankly, close proximity to a man with power on his mind made her want to run in the other direction, as fast as her pink glow-in-the-dark joggers could take her.

It hadn't exactly worked out well for her the last time, had it? Tricked, taken advantage of and publicly dumped, all in the name of career advancement. Michael Unsworth's, to be precise.

Marissa tugged her gold blouse into place over the chocolate skirt and noted Rick's words on her steno pad. *Not noticing him.* Not the charisma, nor the stunning grey eyes fringed with thick black lashes. Certainly not the leashed sensuality that seemed an integral part of him. So totally not noticing any of that.

Anyway, she'd just recently finished telling her Blinddatebrides.com friends Grace and Dani, aka Englishcrumpet and Sanfrandani, about her utter commitment to finding her Mr Ordinary. Though she'd only known Dani and Grace over the Internet a matter of weeks, they were wonderful women and understood and encouraged Marissa's dating goals. She meant to find that Mr Ordinary, to prove to the world... Well, simply to prove she could control her own destiny, thanks very much.

'This bridge isn't a key thoroughfare, Cartwright. It doesn't impact on port access for large seafaring craft.' Rick's strong tanned hand gestured to emphasise his words. 'It isn't a Heritage listed structure and its refurbishment won't make it look like one. The work needs to be about strength, durability and safety in keeping with the established design. The company's initial assessment explained this.'

The bridge spanned two small juts of Sydney's coastline. It rested within the city's sprawling confines but was far from core harbour material. Here there were no stunning views. No Sydney Harbour Bridge. No shell-shaped Opera House rising as though directly from the water.

Unlike Pyrmont, with its massive central swing span, this bridge was just a smallish, nondescript one tucked away on a commercial section of shore.

'You're not listening to what I want.' Cartwright's mouth tightened.

'I've listened. As did the Project Manager who liaised with you initially. The advice in his report was sound.' Overhead, a seagull offered a cry to the pale blue sky as it searched the ocean below for food.

Rick had a strong face to match his strong tone. Wide cheekbones and a firm square jaw that, even at nine-thirty in the morning, revealed a dark beard shadow beneath the skin. A tall vital man with thick shoulders and defined musculature beneath the perfectly cut charcoal suit and pale green shirt.

Marissa didn't want to be aware of him, but she couldn't seem to help it.

'We can make something truly stupendous of this area.' Cartwright repeated his mantra.

Again.

For about the tenth time, paying apparently no attention at all to Rick's explanation.

The company boss growled softly beneath his breath.

It was not a sexy growl!

Marissa inhaled the tang of sea air and Rick's citrusy aftershave cologne and stopped herself from closing her eyes in what would have been a completely inappropriate appreciative sigh.

Instead, she forced her attention to Cartwright's rounded face. Maybe she could help... 'Since you're limited with what you can do in terms of refurbishing this bridge, perhaps you could implement some onshore improvements to emphasise the dock area and make the most of that aspect of things?'

'My thoughts exactly, Marissa. Something more commercially viable.' Rick cast a quick glance her way, offering a small nod of approval. The quirk of his lips that went with that approval made her tummy flutter.

Okay, so the company boss could show appreciation as well as look good. He still fell under the *Tall, Dark and Aggressive about Success* category.

She reminded herself rather desperately that that definition was one hundred per cent not right for her. Despite what her headed-for-thirty-years-of-age and back in the dating pool hormones might suggest otherwise. What did they know, anyway?

Enough to make her join a dating site, and to recognise an appealing man when she saw one?

The first had been a sensible, well-considered decision, nothing more, and, as for the second…

'Not going there,' Marissa muttered towards the foaming sea and tossed her head of curly hair before she remembered the hard hat squashed over the top of it.

Fine, so the impact was lost a little. And she hadn't actually been thinking about emotions. She'd made her choices clinically. That was all she needed to remember. Marissa grimaced and shoved the hat out of her eyes.

'Are you all right?' Rick leaned his head close to hers. The grey of his eyes deepened with a combination of amusement and interest as his gaze roved over the hard hat, her face, the hair sticking out about her cheeks and neck.

'I'm fine, thank you.' He probably wondered why she'd tossed her head like that. 'It was nothing, really. I had a twitch.'

In the brain. It started when I looked into your

eyes this morning as you said, 'Good, you're here,' in that deep, toe-curling voice and it hiccups back every time I look at you or listen to you.

'Er…a twitch that made my head nod and the hat fall forward.'

Toe-curling, *authoritative* voice, Marissa. Get it right if you're going to think it at all.

'I see.' Though his lips didn't move, Rick's eyes smiled.

Marissa stared at that charming expression and thought, *deadly*. The man was deadly to her senses.

'A central steel swing span—' Cartwright began again.

'Would require a whole new bridge, one far larger than this one and located in deeper water.' Rick raised a hand as though to push it through his hair—also covered by a hard hat, except in his case he looked good in it—and dropped it to his side again. 'As Hedley told you in his assessment.'

'Hedley isn't management level,' the man spluttered. 'He doesn't understand some of the committee members' vision for the project. We could have the bridge swing open and closed at certain times of the day—a ceremonial thing even if only smaller craft passed through. It could create a major tourist attraction.'

'But you don't have the funds or planning permission to make that kind of change,' Rick pointed out gently, 'nor the conditions or traffic to demand it.'

'I have influence where the approval is concerned.' Cartwright suddenly turned to glare in Marissa's direction. 'Are you getting all this, girly? I don't see that pen moving.'

'It's a stenographer's pencil,' Marissa corrected kindly while Rick's big body stiffened at her side. 'I've written down every new piece of information you've provided and, actually, I'm almost thirty. Not quite a "girly" any more.'

'*Miss Warren* is part of the Morgan's team. She is not—'

'Not at all perturbed,' Marissa inserted while a flow of gratified warmth filled her.

Rick drew a breath. His gaze locked with hers and the starch left him. His voice dipped about an octave as he murmured, 'Well, you really don't look...'

'That old?' She meant her response to sound cheerful, unconcerned. Instead, it came out with a breathless edge, the result of that considering gaze on her. Of the way he had championed her, despite never having worked directly with her until today.

And perhaps a little because of her need not to feel quite as ancient as she did in the face of her looming birthday. 'Thank you for thinking so.'

Thank you very, very much and you look appealing yourself. Very appealing.

Did hormones have voices? Whispery ones that piped up right when they were least welcome?

First chance we get, Marissa thought, those hormones and I are having a Come To Mama meeting and I'm telling them who's in charge of this show. Namely, me.

Stupid birthdays, anyway. They should be cancelled after twenty-five and never referred to again.

You'll have found Mr Right by your birthday and won't have time to notice that over a third of your estimated life span has passed you by while you wasted some of it on Michael Unsworth, the cheating, lying, using—

'Well. What was it we were saying?' Marissa forced a smile. She mustn't think of Michael, *or* of Rick Morgan's charismatic presence.

'We were discussing this bridge...' Prosaic

words but Rick's gaze moved over her with a delicious consciousness before it was quickly masked.

He was attracted to her!

Her hormones cheered.

Marissa frowned.

He couldn't be attracted. At all. Why would he be?

A moment later he blinked that consciousness away and turned to stare at the other man. 'Unless you have something new to add to the discussion, Cartwright, perhaps we could wind this up.'

Focusing on work was a great idea, really. If her heart had already done a little flip-flop dance, well, that didn't matter. She would simply force all systems back into submission because control was the thing.

Control her destiny and it couldn't hurt—*control*—her, and that was exactly how she wanted things to be.

Rick cleared his throat. 'Mr Cartwright, your committee members will have my report before your eleven o'clock meeting this morning.'

'There's no need to send it to everyone. I'll deliver it at the meeting.' The man actually seemed to believe that Rick would agree to this.

'I assure you, it will be no trouble to see the report into the hands of the whole committee.' Deep voice. Steel-edged politeness.

Marissa had arrived at work this morning expecting to be stultifyingly bored with office filing for at least the next several days. Instead, Rick's secretary had propped himself up in her doorway and croaked out his request that she meet his boss on site so he could take himself off to the doctor.

Next minute Marissa had been whipping along in a taxi, and then she'd found Rick waiting for her at the bridge site like a knight in shining hard hat.

Well, not really a knight. No horse. But he'd listened patiently as she'd given a flurried explanation to go with her sudden appearance, then he'd said, 'Yes, I know. Shall we?' and had cupped her elbow to escort her onto the bridge.

That constituted contact, which was why she could blame this entire blip in her reaction to him on her senses, not her intellect.

Rick went on, 'The report will explain why your ideas won't work, and will agree with my assessor's initial report and recommend the committee works directly with him from now on. Had there not been a temp from downstairs manning my office the day you made your appointment, you'd have been informed that you should meet with the Project Manager today, not me.'

Having a temp make an inappropriate appointment for him explained how Rick had ended up wasting his time on this meeting. Marissa had wondered. Her attraction to him didn't explain anything, except her hormones apparently hadn't read her Blinddatebrides profile or her list of requirements in a prospective mate.

Date. Prospective date. And this man wasn't one. She expected all of her to take note.

'You'll be billed for this discussion. I hope your interactions with our company will remain amicable and be a little more focused in the future.' Having made it plain that the man's efforts to bypass the proper channels hadn't come free of charge, Rick nodded. 'Now, if you'll excuse us.'

Good. It was over. They could get back to the office and Marissa could forget this weird awareness of the boss and return to her real work. In this instance, taking care of the backlog of filing Gordon had left behind before he'd gone on holiday and, once that was done, a long list of non-urgent hack work he'd left for her.

Rick's firm fingers wrapped around her elbow. Instant overload.

Nerve-endings. Senses. Her gaze flew to his. He was already watching her. His fingers tightened.

For a frozen heartbeat his gaze became very intent indeed. Then he shook his head and swept her away along the bridge and she started to breathe again and reminded herself of her focus.

Nice. Ordinary. Guy.

Someone to have babies with. If they wanted to. At some point when they decided they'd like that. No rush at all. Again, Marissa was the leader of this particular outfit, not her clock or her hormones or anything else.

She frowned. What did she mean, *clock*? As in ticking biological clock? How silly. She simply wanted someone steady and dependable and completely invested in building a solid relationship of trust, friendship and affection with her.

Sure, that might mean a family one day, but she didn't feel driven to have children. Just because she found herself noticing mothers with babies in supermarkets and shops and on the street…

No. The Big 3-0 didn't stand for B. A. B. Y.

Not at all.

It only stood for birthday-she-didn't-want-to-think-about.

Hmph.

And just because she'd noticed the Morgan's boss...

'Tom explained he was unwell before he sent you out here to meet me?' Rick spoke the words as he steered her along. 'Did he give you his travel pack?'

'I met with Tom briefly at the office before his wife whisked him away to go to the doctor.' Marissa tapped the bag that slapped against her hip with each step.

Rick must be around six foot two inches tall. Much of it appeared to be strong, ground-eating legs, not that she wanted to think about his legs, or even his anatomy in general. 'And, yes, I have Tom's travel pack.'

The shoes that went so nicely with her chocolate-brown knee-length skirt were also shoved in the tote.

'You'll need it for dictation on the trip back to the office.' He hit the base of the bridge without slowing his pace, though he took care to make sure she could keep up.

As he walked forward he dropped his hold on her and drew out his mobile phone. The conversation when the number picked up brought an edge of concern to his face and deepened the grooves on either side of his firm, moulded lips.

Would those grooves crease appealingly when he smiled?

Not interested in the answer to that. Not interested in the lips that would form the smile, or the abandoned feeling in one particular elbow either.

'You'll recover, though?… What's the treatment?… Can Linda get some time off work? If she can't, I'll arrange nursing care for you.' He listened for a moment and some of the tension in his face eased. 'Okay. You've got it covered then, but if you think of anything you need, you let me know, and don't worry about work. I'll cope.'

He paused. His grey gaze examined her, frankly assessing her before he spoke again. 'It wasn't your fault I ended up at this meeting this morning, Tom. We agreed to put a temp in the chair that day and she apparently didn't know any better than to book me for this appointment instead of the Project Manager. Cartwright took advantage of that fact.'

The second pause lasted longer, or maybe it felt that way because his gaze stayed on her the whole time. 'Yes, I know and I suppose you're right. I'd had the same thought.' His tone softened. 'Now let Linda put you to bed, man. I'll check in with her later.'

Before Marissa could get all mushy over that obvious concern for his employee, or feel uneasy as a result of his focus on her, he closed the phone.

'Is Tom—?' She got that far with the question before he brought them to a halt beside a large slate-coloured four-wheel-drive car.

People called them *cars*. Marissa told herself this was a muscular extension of its owner. All strong lines and height and breadth and power. It was twice as tall as an ordinary car, and it should stand as a warning to her. There was no softness to be found here, no gentler side, just sheer strength.

Really? Because Rick had *seemed* quite considerate, as well as all those other things.

'Tom is ill with what appears to be a hard-hitting virus. Ross River fever, the doctor thinks.' Rick removed his hard hat and ran his hand through his hair for real. Thick dark hair with a glint or two of silver at the temples. He was thirty-seven years old, her boss Gordon had told her, with degrees in both civil engineering and architecture.

Rick had used those and other skills to forge his way to massive success consulting on structural refurbishment and undertaking new construction work. Bridges, buildings, roads, he'd covered all of it and now had a team of several hundred people working under him, just in the office side of his business alone.

That was what Marissa needed to remember. The word 'driven' probably didn't begin to describe him.

Driven. Willing to do anything to get what he wanted, no matter how that impacted on others? Like Michael Unsworth?

'Ross River fever can be quite debilitating while it lasts, can't it? Tom did look very unwell this morning.' Marissa had worried for the man until he'd assured her that his wife would soon be there to collect him. She didn't want her thoughts on Rick, and she pursued the conversation with that in mind. 'I hope Tom recovers quickly and fully.'

'Linda will make sure he rests, and I'll be

keeping an eye on his progress…' He used the remote on his keyring to unlock his car. Even the movement of those strong, long-fingered hands appealed.

'I'm glad I could fill in for Tom this morning, though the meeting turned out to be a bit of a waste of time for you.' Marissa wrestled with the strap of her hard hat and finally got the thing off. Wrestled to get her thoughts into submission at the same time. A quick shake of her head took care of any hat hair possibility, though she knew that nothing would keep her curls down for long.

'I appreciated that you got yourself here quickly when Tom couldn't. Make sure you hand your taxi receipt in for reimbursement.' He had his hand out, reaching to open the passenger door. It paused mid-stretch as his gaze locked onto her head and stark male awareness flared in the backs of his eyes. 'Your hair—'

'Is it a mess? I'm afraid I can't do a whole lot with it, though I do occasionally tie it back or put it up.' She uttered the words while she tried to come to terms with the expression in his eyes, with the reciprocal burst of interest it raised in her. Goosebumps tingled over her nape and down her arm. 'It's just that it takes ages and I was busy this morning,' she finished rather lamely while she fought not to notice those re-actions.

'"Mess" wasn't really what I was thinking.' He murmured the admission as though against his will, and then, 'Let me have the hat.' His fingers brushed hers as he took it from her.

Warmth flowed back up her arm again from the brief contact.

Totally immune to him, are we? Doesn't look like it, and he definitely did *notice you just now. You saw it for yourself.*

Oh, shut up!

He tossed the hats onto the back seat and ushered her towards the front one. 'Hop in. This was my third stop this morning. I have quite a bit of dictation for the trip back to the office. It's up to you whether you speak your notes into a recorder or write them down, but there are deals in progress, so we need to get moving.'

'I'm quite willing to be occupied.' *And you see?* The Morgan's boss *was* highly focused on his work, his success. All those things Michael had cared the most about, had used her to achieve. Marissa hopped, or rather, he boosted her up into the high cab of the car and she landed in the seat with a bit of a plop. It was a soft, comfortable, welcoming seat, contrasting with the strength of the vehicle itself.

Not that she thought Rick Morgan had a soft side to match his car. She couldn't let herself think that. He was off-limits to her in any case and she needed her hormones to accept that fact without any further pointless comparisons.

The manoeuvre had also left rather a lot of leg exposed and she quickly tugged the skirt back into place.

Rick's gaze locked onto that expanse of leg and he caught his breath. Blinked twice. And then he strode around the front of the vehicle with his shoulders thrown back and a shuttered expression on his face that made her more conscious of him than ever.

He couldn't want her. In fact he was probably wondering why on earth he had noticed her at all. She would seem like part of the furniture to him. Like a coffee table with sturdy blocks keeping it low to the ground. Well, women her height didn't have slender legs that went on for ever, did they? Not that she was comparing herself to a coffee table.

'I'll take written notes.' She didn't want to

speak aloud in front of him for who knew how long, repeating everything he said. That would feel far too intim—*uncomfortable*. 'It'll be more efficient.'

'Then let's see what we can do about cementing the positive outcomes that are riding on this morning's earlier visits.' He set the car in motion while she prepared herself—a man with power and achievement on his mind.

Michael Unsworth had been all about those things too, in the most arrogant of ways, though it had taken her way too long to see that, to see beyond his surface charm. He'd led her on, taken credit for all her hard work for him as though he'd done it all himself and, when she'd called him on that, he'd dumped her, had claimed their secret engagement had never existed. She was more than over all that, of course. It had happened months ago and she'd told him what a snake he was at the time.

Yes. Totally moved on. Her ongoing tendency to occasionally blare raging *I don't need a man* style music in her apartment at night notwithstanding.

She happened to like the musical accompaniments to some of those particular songs, and if she truly felt that way she wouldn't be trying to find a man she liked on a dating site, would she?

And you don't think you're so keen to find a man because Michael dumped you and your birthday will be the anniversary of the day you believed you and he became 'secretly' engaged as well as making you officially 'old'? You're not out to prove something? Several somethings, in fact?

She was simply out to do something positive and proactive about her future. She didn't even care if she found a man before she turned thirty. The dating site was a way to look around. If nothing eventuated, no big deal.

And this awareness of her boss... Well, it would go away. He might be *somewhat* nice, but that didn't change his corporate status. She would ignore her consciousness of him until it disappeared.

'Yes.' She was ready, under control and safe from the temptation of a corporate boss with power on her mind. Marissa clutched her pencil and hoped that was true!

CHAPTER TWO

RICK turned his car into the traffic and started to dictate. First came the report for Cartwright's committee meeting. Then a bunch of short memos to be emailed to various department heads regarding the other projects he had visited this morning. Marissa's pencil flew across the pages while she remained utterly conscious of his presence at her side.

In the confines of the big car she registered each breath and movement as he managed the congested traffic conditions with ease. Maybe joining a dating site had raised her overall awareness of men in a general sense?

That might explain this sudden inconvenient fixation on Rick.

He paused, glanced at her. 'All right? Are you keeping up?'

'Yes.' She waved the hand with the pencil in it and didn't let on for a moment that it ached somewhat from the thorough workout. 'Gordon always dictates when we're out on site work.'

Which had been all of three or four times since she'd started with her middle-aged boss six months ago, and Gordon always paused to ponder between each sentence.

'Take this list down then, please.' Rick went on to give a prioritised outline of workaday items— phone calls to be made, documentation to be lifted from files and information to be gathered from other departments within the company.

He had crow's feet at the corners of his eyes. They crinkled when he scrunched his face in thought or gave that slight smile, and made him look even better. Gorgeous, with character.

Whereas Marissa had spent over a hundred dollars on a miracle fine line facial cream last week, an action that had puzzled the younger of her Blinddatebrides friends Dani, and made Grace laugh, albeit rather wryly.

When Rick wound up his dictation, she gestured at the steno pad now crammed with instructions. 'Someone's going to be busy. There's also a BlackBerry in the pack Tom gave me. Do you want me to read you the day's list?'

In case he'd missed something in the estimated

ten hours of straight work he'd just hammered out for whoever got the job of replacing Tom in his absence? She pitied those girls in the general pool on the first floor. Maybe he'd take two of them. Not her problem, in any case.

After this trip, Marissa would take her fine line wrinkles and go back to Gordon's office.

Rick probably wouldn't be in a good mood about the first floor help, though, given his last temp from there had booked an appointment for him to go out on a matter someone else should have handled.

'Yes, check through and see what I've missed, would you?' He signalled, slowed and turned and she realised with a start that they were back at their North Sydney office building. The city pulsed with busyness around them before he took the car underground, but she could only focus on *his* busyness.

Note to self about go-getter busyness, Marissa: it is not an endearing or invigorating trait.

She quickly pulled the electronic organiser from Tom's travel pack in her tote. Scanned. Read. Tried not to acknowledge the burst of irrational disappointment that swept through her.

'There's a notation of "Julia" for twelve-thirty.' He wouldn't hear the slight uneven edge in her tone, would he? How silly to care that he was seeing someone. She should have realised that would be the case. It shouldn't matter to her that he was! 'That's the only thing listed that you haven't brought up.'

Of course the listing *could* be for any reason. Hairdresser appointment. An hour with his gym trainer. Or a pet schnauzer he walked faithfully once a day.

Dream on, Marissa.

'Ah, yes.' His face softened for a moment before he turned into his parking space and opened his door.

A go-getting corporate shark who had no business noticing the help if he was already involved. Probably with some sophisticated woman, maybe the daughter of a fellow businessman, or a corporate high-flyer herself. She'd be stunningly beautiful and *her* face cream would work like a charm, if she needed it at all.

You're being ridiculous. He barely noticed you in passing and he certainly didn't seem thrilled once he realised he had. Nor do you want to be thrilled or notice him.

Marissa released her seat belt, shoved the PDA back into her tote bag and drew out her work shoes.

With her head bent removing the joggers, she said in what she felt was a perfectly neutral tone, 'Feel free to go on ahead. I can either stop by the first floor general pool for you and ask them to send someone up, or bring the PDA and my notes to whoever you've chosen to replace Tom. You can pre-lock this monster so I just have to shut the door, I assume?'

'Thanks for the kind offer.' Rick watched as Marissa Warren pushed a second trim foot into a shapely shoe. She had beautiful ankles. And legs. And a sweetness in her face that had tugged unexpectedly at something deep inside him from the moment he'd seen her up close for the first time this morning.

He'd noticed her in the office, of course. He noticed all the staff. As owner and manager, it was part of his job to remain aware about who worked for him, though the company was so big nowadays and employed so many people that he didn't always have anything specific to do with some of the workers.

In any case Marissa was completely unsuitable

as a woman he should notice, legs or not. He wasn't prepared to risk commitment and the failure that could go with it, and he didn't tangle with the kind of women who might want it. Marissa struck him as a woman who would want all sorts of pieces of a man that Rick might not have the ability to give. Not that he'd ever wanted to.

'I'll wait for you.'

She didn't realise yet there would be no parting. But this didn't have to be about anything beyond work requirements. And, ultimately, he didn't have a whole lot of better options.

'If you insist,' she muttered, and pushed her joggers into her tote bag.

Why he couldn't seem to take his gaze from her, he simply couldn't explain. Yet she'd drawn his attention from the moment she'd arrived at the bridge, that hard hat rammed down on her head like armour plating.

Most of the women in the office were either in their forties or fifties, married and/or otherwise committed, or giggling twenty-year-olds. Marissa didn't fit either of those groups. She didn't seem the type to giggle.

Maybe that explained this odd attraction to Gordon Slaymore's secretary.

Rick got out, closed his door, moved to her side and pulled hers open. 'Ready?'

'Yes. It was kind of you to wait, though unnecessary.' She stood at about five foot five inches in height with a compact body that curved in all the right places. Brown eyes sparkled one moment and seemed to guard secrets the next and that wealth of hair caressed her face and nape in all its curly wildness. Her nose was strong and straight, her mouth soft and inviting in a girl-next-door kind of way.

He shouldn't want to know about the guardedness or cheerfulness. Definitely needed to steer clear of the girl-next-door part. 'Let's go, then.'

'Right.' She would have got down without touching him. The intention to do so flared in her eyes.

Given the way he reacted the few times they'd touched, he should have allowed exactly that but some bizarre sense of perversity made him clasp her hand and help her. Then, because he didn't want to release his hold on her, wanted to stroke that hand with his fingertips, he dropped it altogether, closed the door and locked the vehicle.

He wanted to kiss her until they were both breathless from it, and when she joined him in the lift the urge to do that came very close to overwhelming him.

While he fought urges he usually had no difficulty controlling, Marissa reached out a small, capable-looking hand towards the panel. No doubt to press for the first floor and the help she thought he wanted.

Instead, he pushed the button that would take them directly to his floor, and thought how he would like to taste those softly pouting lips.

This wasn't happening. It *didn't* happen to him. He was no green youngster who reacted this way to a woman. He'd found her easy enough not to notice until now and he planned to go on not noticing her.

'Gordon's on holiday.' The abrupt announcement wasn't exactly his usual smooth delivery, but at least it got them back onto a business footing. 'You probably only had maintenance and catch-up work planned, you have some experience behind you and can keep up with my pace of dictation. I've decided it will be best if you assist me during Tom's sick leave.'

'You want *me*?' An expression rather close to

horror flashed across her face before she quickly concealed it.

'I don't imagine I'll find anyone any better qualified and as easily available as you are.' He'd meant to state the words in a calm, if decided way. Instead they almost sounded bewildered. And perhaps a little insulted. He had to admit that her reaction had been refreshingly honest and appeared to come straight from her heart. Emotional honesty hadn't exactly been abundant from some of the people in his life.

And just where had that unhelpful thought come from? A very old place!

After a moment she murmured, 'Well, I'm sure it won't be for long.'

The grudging acceptance wasn't exactly effusive and it left him wanting to…impress her with how amenable he could be as a boss.

'Gordon has four weeks off, doesn't he?' Rick pushed away his odd reaction and forced his attention to matters close to hand. 'I seem to recall that from a brief talk I had with him before he left. I'm sure that will allow more than enough time for Tom to recuperate and return. If not, we'll simply deal with it. You can make whatever arrangements are needed to replace yourself in Gordon's office.

Put a temp in there and have the first floor supervisor monitor the temp's progress.'

'Yes, of course. I didn't meant to sound... Well, I was just surprised, that's all.'

Oh, she'd meant it, but he pushed that aside too.

'Then, if you have no other questions...?' He paused and she shook her head. 'Good. We'll just get on with it, then.'

With his unwelcome awareness of her firmly set aside and filed, he whisked her out of the lift and into the hub of his work.

He would simply rein in his odd response to her and they would get along just fine.

Expediency. It was all about what was best for the company.

CHAPTER THREE

To: Sanfrandani, Englishcrumpet
From: Kangagirl
I had to cancel the after-hours second drink with the bank clerk guy. Work issues. I've been roped in to work for the big boss for the next while. Totally out of my control and since I don't know how long things will be busy and the bank clerk might want to see other women in the meantime, I didn't ask him to reschedule. Still, it looks like there will be one or two perks with this temporary job. I peeked ahead in the BlackBerry and we have a special meeting scheduled for tomorrow, a group of Asian businessmen. We're taking them to an animal petting zoo.

From: Sanfrandani
Ooh. What sort of animals?

From: Englishcrumpet
Kangaroos? I've always wanted to see one of those. I hope the different work goes well for you, Marissa.

'What did his last servant die of? I wonder.' Marissa muttered as her fingers flew at lightning speed to produce yet another memo that needed to be rushed urgently to one of their departments.

She absolutely did *not* enjoy the pace and challenge of working in Rick's sumptuous office suite with its thick beige carpet and burnished gold walls and stunning view over Sydney Harbour. And its frenetic pace. Maybe this workload was why Tom had gone down with a virus.

Except Ross River virus wasn't something one contracted due to stress. And the company boss did *not* fascinate Marissa more and more with each breath she took. He wasn't tremendously adept at his work, and appealingly sexy as he went about it. He was…obsessed by it. Yes, that was it.

He'd probably prove to be a terrible boss, never giving the poor overworked secretary a second thought after that initial consideration.

And *she'd* refused to look his way for at least the last five minutes, anyway, so there.

Rick dropped another pile of papers and three tapes into her tray. 'You're coping all right? Not feeling too pressured? I know there's a lot of work, but we can take things steadily.' His gaze caught and held hers with quiet sincerity.

Which rather shot holes in her thoughts about him. She was far better off viewing him as a workaholic quite prepared to take her down with him! 'I'm managing. Thank you.'

He lingered in front of her desk for a moment and his gaze moved from her hands to her face and hair before coming back to her eyes. For one still moment she couldn't seem to look away and he...didn't seem to be able to either. Then he cleared his throat. 'That report hit the right places before eleven a.m.?'

'Report...' Oh, yes. Right. Well, he'd proofed the thing just minutes ago and she'd sent it. Except...Marissa forced her gaze from him to the square-framed clock on the far wall of the office space and realised it was now twelve twenty-five.

'I faxed the report on time to each committee member. You must be due for your lunch appointment.' *She* must be due to remember he had that appointment, and what that meant. The man was not available. There was Julia in his life, not that Marissa imagined *herself* in Rick Morgan's life. Not in that way.

He doesn't have a photo of a woman on his desk.

Maybe he carries it in his wallet, or has it tattooed on his right biceps.

Oh, for crying out loud!

'We'll start again at one-thirty. Your meals can go on my account at the cafeteria while you're working for me, unless you prefer to eat elsewhere.' He simply announced this, in the same way any generous, thoughtful employer taking care of his employee would. 'If you need anything from your desk in Gordon's office get it as quickly as you can when you come back from your break.'

Right, and she was finished with fantasising about tattooed biceps too. *Julia. Remember Julia?*

'We're in for overtime, aren't we?' She asked it with an edge of desperation as she popped up out of her seat. The movement had nothing to do with feeling needed and energised and as though

Rick wouldn't be able to function as well without her help. She wanted a lunch break, that was all.

She'd travelled the 'feeling needed' road already, hadn't she? The indispensable-secret-fiancée road until Michael Unsworth had no longer needed her slaving away on his behalf.

The smile on her face dissolved at the thought. She snagged her tote bag and headed for the office door. 'I will eat at the cafeteria. I often do, anyway. Have a lovely time with Julia.'

'Thank you.' He let her walk to the door before he spoke again. 'Could you bring me back two beef and salad rolls and a bottle of orange juice after your meal? I won't actually be eating lunch while I'm gone.'

Again, there could be a hundred reasons for that. Only one flashed through her mind, though, and to her mortification her face became red-hot as a barrage of uninvited images paraded through her clearly incorrectly functioning brain.

'Certainly.' She bolted through the door and promised herself she would dedicate her entire lunch break to locating and lassoing her common sense and control, and tying them down where they belonged. 'I'll see that the meal is waiting when you return.'

She did exactly that after eating a sensible salad lunch that wouldn't get her hips into trouble and she didn't think about her boss. Not once. Not at all. She was a professional and she didn't give a hoot what Rick did with his time.

Marissa followed up this thought by rushing from the building to the convenience store situated at the end of the block. It was perfectly normal to buy an entire six-pack of raspberry lemonade and just because that was her comfort drink of choice didn't mean anything. Bulk was cheaper.

With a huff Marissa turned from placing the drinks in the fridge in the suite's kitchenette beside the boss's lunch and OJ and made her way to Gordon's office.

There'd be a temp tomorrow. For today the general pool was a little short-staffed so the office was silent as she collected the framed photo of her Mum and Dad taken last year just after they'd downsized into their two-bedroom home in Milberry, and a small tray full of bits and pieces—nail files, amazing hand cream to go with the amazing face cream, breath mints.

She also picked up the laminate of cartoon

cuttings she'd collated a few months ago—cheery ones, joky ones, sarcasm about pets and life and getting up in the mornings. It made an entertaining desktop addition and there was no significance to the fact that she had avoided any cartoons to do with ageing.

Everyone got a day older each time they rolled out of bed in the morning. That was life. It was certainly no big deal to her. And she'd left off cartoons about babies, children and families because…this was a laminate she'd wanted for work, and those things didn't fit into that world.

And the fact that you purchased a pair of baby-gauge knitting needles recently and two balls of baby-soft wool?

It had been an impulse buy. One of those things you did and then wondered why you had. Besides, she hadn't bought any knitting patterns to go with the wool and, if she did decide to use it, she'd knit herself a pair of socks or something.

She would!

Back in her new office, Marissa shoved the laminate onto the left half of the desk and quickly buried it beneath her in-tray and various piles of folders, typed letters and other work.

When her boss walked in and fell on the lunch she'd brought as though starved to death, Marissa kept on with her work and didn't spare him a glance. If she had a 'spare' anything, she would invest it thinking about which man she might date next off the Blinddatebrides website.

Silly name, really, because she wasn't desperate for marriage or anything like that. They'd had a special on and there were lots of nice everyday men out there, and her thirtieth birthday *wasn't looming*.

It was still weeks away, even if Mum had fallen eerily silent about it, the way she did when she got the idea to spring a surprise on her daughter. Marissa didn't want a surprise party— or any kind of party—and she hoped her Mum had understood that from her hints on the topic.

There was no big deal about wanting to find a man before she turned thirty anyway, and nor was Marissa's pride in a mess because she'd been duped and dumped.

She had her whole world in complete control, and she liked it just fine that way!

'Good afternoon, Rick Morgan's office, this is Marissa.'

Rick sat at his desk and listened as Marissa

answered yet another phone call and took a message. He'd told her he didn't want to be disturbed while he worked his way through the report that had been delivered.

Yet he hadn't managed to tune out his awareness of her as she beavered away at her desk.

Maybe it was the way her hands flew across the computer keys that had him glancing her way over and over. Or the fact that when she thought herself unobserved her interest in the materials she processed showed all over her expressive face.

Frowns and nods of approval came into play until she finally printed out each piece of work with an expression of satisfaction. Would she be as open and responsive—?

That wasn't something he needed to know, yet the thought was there, along with others. Rick finished reading the report and scooped up the signed letters that needed to be mailed.

'You like hard work, don't you.' It wasn't really a question but he set the signed letters down on the corner of her desk and waited for her to answer anyway. That was another problem he appeared to have developed. He couldn't seem to stop himself from getting up from his desk and finding a reason to visit hers.

Once there, his gaze seemed to have a will of its own, roving constantly over her face and hair, the nape of her neck, the hands that moved with such speed and efficiency over the computer keyboard. He wanted those hands on him.

No. He did *not* want Marissa Warren's hands on him. Yet there was something between them. It had been there from the moment they'd met at the bridge this morning and he'd let her come to the most predictable conclusion about Julia because of that.

Now he wanted to explain, wanted her to know he was free—but he wasn't, was he? Not to get involved with his temporary secretary, or any other woman who wanted more than a casual physical interlude with him. He'd made his choice about that.

'Do I like hard work?' Her gaze flipped up to his. Almost immediately she veiled the sparkle in her eyes. A shrug of one shoulder followed. 'I guess I like to think I'm as efficient as the next person and there seems a lot to be done in this office at the moment. Or perhaps it's always this busy?'

'Tom and I work hard, but there's more to contend with right now than is usual, even for us.' To move his gaze from her, he shifted it to a photo of an older couple that she'd added to her desk. The woman had curly hair, cut shorter. Her parents…

Was she an only child or did she, like him, have siblings? An intriguing-looking laminated sheet covered the left half of the desk. Much of it had work strewn on top but the bits he could see appeared to be cartoon cuttings.

Her foibles and family history shouldn't interest him. Another sign of trouble, and yet still he stood here, courting time with her when both their interests would be better served if he didn't.

'Will it be a problem for you to work longer hours for the next few days?' That was what he really needed to know. 'Is there someone at home who'll mind?'

Marissa's answer was only relevant to him in terms of how it impacted here.

Except his body stilled as he waited for her response, and that stillness had little to do with concerns about his working life.

'Tom has welcomed the longer hours because he and Linda are saving to buy a house.' The words left his mouth in an explanation he hadn't intended to give. 'He's used to my ways and knows his way around this office. He copes.'

'I can manage any work Tom would have done.' She spoke the words with her chin in the air. An answer, but not all the information he had wanted.

'I don't doubt that.' He wanted her to know he thought well of her. Wanted her to…think well of him. The last time he'd experienced this particular care about another's opinion of him, he'd been twenty years old and convinced he was in love, until the girl had started talking about the future—theirs—and he'd wanted to run a mile.

Just like his father, except Stephen Morgan was *in a family* and he did his running a little differently. Rick hadn't even tried for a less than overt approach. He'd got out of that relationship so fast he'd probably left the girl spinning and he'd avoided commitment ever since.

'I'm not…tied to any home responsibilities.' Marissa offered this information cautiously, as though she'd prefer not to have given it.

'Then I won't worry too much if I do have to ask you to work extra hours.' Rick stared into the warm brown eyes fixed unerringly on him and the moment stretched out, expanded to encompass not only the words they had exchanged but also what they weren't saying. The sparkle in the air between them. His awareness of her, hers of him, the denial of both of them.

Sexual attraction. That was all it was, but even so it wasn't wise and he *had* to realise that and move them past it. He drew a deep breath. 'It's clear you can cope with the workload. You've handled yourself very well so far today. I appreciate your efforts.'

'Th-thank you.' A pleased expression lifted the corners of her mouth and softened her eyes. 'I've simply done my job.'

Something about that softening brought back the urge he'd had earlier in the lift to kiss her senseless, and he lowered his tone of voice to a low rumble. 'So I've observed.'

'I can work whatever hours are needed. I'd just appreciate knowing so I can gear my social life accordingly.' She cleared her throat and couldn't quite seem to meet his gaze. 'I cancelled a drink after work today because I figured I wouldn't be out by five.'

Rick wanted to say there'd be no time whatsoever for her to spend on 'drinks'. Presumably with some man. He noted at the same time that she must be looking. Looking, but not seriously involved right now.

But women who looked and carried photos of their parents with them did want depth and permanency, and that kind of relationship was not on his agenda.

'I should get on, if that was all.' She reached for the pile of letters to be mailed, began to calmly fold them into the window envelopes she had waiting on her desk.

Dismissed by his temporary assistant. Rick gave a snort of amusement and reluctant admiration before he swung away. 'I'll be in my office and...er...I promise there won't be any more correspondence brought out for you to type today. I know your tray is still loaded.'

'No.' She didn't look up. 'You'll just hold it over for tomorrow so I won't get stressed out. I won't anyway, but that's okay. I understand the tactic. Gordon does the same thing.'

Now he'd been compared to a fifty-year-old.

Rick disappeared into his office, pushed the door closed so he wouldn't be tempted to listen to Marissa taking phone calls or watch her as she worked, and decided that it was very different working with her rather than Tom.

That explained his ongoing interest in her. He half convinced himself he believed this. Well, maybe a quarter. He immersed himself in his work.

At twenty minutes to six that evening Marissa stuck her head around his door. 'Your presence is requested at an emergency conference.'

He'd started to believe they might have nearly caught up on their workload. So much for that idea. 'Which department heads? What's the problem?'

She pushed the door open fully and read a spiel of information from her steno pad.

Rick gave a mild curse. 'Where? Have they assembled already?'

'Conference Room Two, and yes.' She had her tote bag on her shoulder and a determined glint in her eyes. Her computer was shut down and her desk cleared. Whatever work she had remaining she had tidied away. 'I assume you'll want us to join them immediately. If it ends quickly, we can come back.'

He got to his feet. 'I'll secure my office.'

She swept in beside him while he sorted files and locked them away. 'Anything on screen that needs to be saved before I shut this down?'

'No. Nothing, but I can do that.' He locked the final cabinet and swung round.

She'd clicked out of applications as he spoke and she stood there now, bent at the waist, leaning in to press the button on the back of the computer.

Rick's senses kicked him hard. She would have to possess the most appealing bottom to go with those equally devastating legs, wouldn't she? And he would have to notice it instead of being completely unaware of her, as he needed to be. He didn't want to notice her, or be impressed or intrigued by her or find her different or interesting or highly attractive!

If he'd thought it would help, he'd replace her with someone from another department but no other personal secretary had a boss on holiday. He certainly wasn't about to subject himself to some child from the general pool again. And, for goodness' sake, he could control this.

He always controlled the way he reacted to women. There was no reason why this situation should be any different. In fact, because she worked for him and he never, ever, mixed work with his social interactions that way, it should be easier still.

Yes, and it's been dead easy so far, hasn't it?

'Let's move.' He hid a grimace in his chin. 'Here's hoping the meeting doesn't go on too long.'

CHAPTER FOUR

MARISSA followed Rick along the corridor and tried not to look at the breadth of his shoulders, the shape of the back of his head or…other parts of him.

Not to mention the man was seriously compelling as a go-getter businessman…but what was she thinking? The terms 'go-getter', 'businessman' and 'compelling' were mutually exclusive in her vocabulary!

And just because he'd been kind to his secretary and had phoned in again to check on the man and declared he wanted to be told if anything—*anything*—needed to be done for Tom while he was recuperating, just because he'd treated Marissa herself with the utmost consideration he could manage within the demands of his work…

She still wanted a *nice ordinary guy*—hello? Fine, so maybe Rick did have a degree of niceness. His career outlook made him totally out of bounds for her.

Maybe he's a total playboy, she thought with a hint of desperation, remembering the Julia lunch date that hadn't involved lunch. A cad, a womaniser, a toad on a lily pad on a pond full of scum.

You don't think you're judging him ever so slightly on Michael Unsworth's record without getting to know the man first? Without even knowing just who this Julia is to him?

No. She didn't think that, and she wasn't grasping at mental straws to keep her hormones under control either. Rick Morgan wasn't for her. She'd road-tested one corporate man and decided that brand didn't suit her, and that was all there was to it.

'Sit here beside me.' He held the chair for her while the six men in the room glanced their way. 'You know what to do with the notes.'

She nodded to acknowledge the others' presence and Rick's words, and tried not to notice the brush of his hand against her back as he pushed her chair in for her.

The boss simply had nice manners, and so did a lot of accountants and shop assistants.

Butchers and bakers and candlestick-makers.
Marissa jabbed her pencil onto the page and locked her gaze onto its tip. 'I'm ready.'

To get the meeting over with. To go home for the day and log onto Blinddatebrides.com and read at least ten new profiles, answer any invitations she'd received and be really positive about them. And she had been positive to this point. It wasn't her fault if no spark of true interest had happened when she'd met any of her dates so far.

Unlike the spark that immediately happened when she'd met Rick Morgan.

Not a helpful thought!

The meeting went beyond long.

'So we find a way to meet the changes to the fire safety code without compromising on design integrity.' Rick referred to a skyscraper monstrosity the company was building on the city's shoreline. 'We'll simply present our clients with choices that surpass what they wanted initially.'

He raised several possibilities. While general discussion ensued, Marissa snatched at the momentary respite in note-taking. She should have eaten something more substantial than a salad for her lunch. Instead, she drew one of two bottles of raspberry lemonade from her tote bag and consumed half of it in a series of swallows. She'd planned to take both bottles in her bag home but at least it gave her an energy burst.

The conference moved on. Marissa consumed the rest of the drink, continued her work. Wished she could get up and walk around. Her right foot wanted to go to sleep. Another sign of impending old age?

There is no old age occurring here!

'It seems to me Phil's presented you with a workable resolution to the issue with the reservoir, Fred.' Rick caught the stare of the man at the other end of the oval table.

Marissa vaguely noted that Rick's beard shadow had really grown in now. Did he shave twice a day? Would he have a mat of dark hair on his chest as well? Her skin tingled in response to the thought.

What was wrong with her? She needed to focus *away* from the man, not so solidly on him that she noticed almost everything about him and wondered about the rest!

Rick's face showed no sign of fatigue, though

the grooves on either side of his mouth did seem a little deeper.

It wasn't fair that men just developed character while women fought gravity. Women wrinkled sooner, got older faster. And people had coined entire sayings around the thirtieth birthday. *It's all downhill after thirty...*

'If you don't want to accept the plans,' Rick went on, 'I need to hear a good reason for that. Otherwise, I think we can move onto the next issue.'

Marissa nodded in silent agreement.

Just then Rick glanced her way and their gazes locked before his dropped to her mouth. He stilled and a single swift blast of awareness swept over his face and, very, very briefly, he lost his concentration and stopped speaking.

It was only for a second and probably no one else would have thought anything of it, but in that single moment she had all of his attention— an overwhelming degree of attention, as though he could *only* focus on her. And, right down to her marrow, she responded with a depth of warmth and interest, curiosity and compulsion that...stunned her.

A moment later his face smoothed of all expression and he carried on with the meeting, and Marissa did her best to pull herself together.

Her lungs chose to function again after all, and she sucked in a deep breath and couldn't— simply couldn't—think about the strength of the response he'd drawn from her just then.

A burst of note-taking followed and when it ended she gulped down the second bottle of lemonade and tapped her foot incessantly. It was almost a relief to focus on her exhaustion and discomfort.

'Anything else?' Rick sent the words down the length of the table. He wanted the conference over with. It was eight p.m. and his secretary was wilting, her fluffy hair sticking out in odd places and the pink lip-gloss, that made him think of snatching kisses, all but chewed off.

Her shoulders were curved, her left elbow propped on the table while she pushed the pencil across the page with grim determination with her other hand.

He had the oddest desire to protect her from the workload he had inflicted on her—even while he'd noted her pleasure in it. He had the oddest desire for her, period. It had stopped his concentration earlier, had simply shut down all channels until he'd pulled his attention forcibly away from her. No person had had the power to disrupt his thoughts so thoroughly before.

It was more than simply a blast of lust, Morgan. Maybe you should admit that to yourself.

Yet what else could it have been? He didn't experience any other feelings. Just look at the way he'd run the one and only time he'd linked up with a woman who wanted more from him. More than his father could give, more than Rick knew if he could give. At least he chose to go forward honestly, not let anyone down…

Around the table, people scooped up folders and files.

Rick nodded. 'Then that's a wrap. Anything else, get it to me in writing tomorrow.'

The room cleared while Marissa continued to write. In the end, he reached out and stilled her hand by placing his over it. Gently, because for some reason she drew that response from him whether he wanted it to be so or not.

Touching her was a mistake. Her skin was warm, soft, and the urge inside him to caress more of it was unexpectedly potent.

Wouldn't his youngest sister gloat about this

fixation of his? Faith had tried to convince him to fall for the 'right kind' of woman for years, to take the leap into emotional oblivion and surrender and believe he'd like it.

What was he thinking, anyway? This was all completely irrelevant. He'd done the not-getting-involved-life-alone mental adjustment years before and he hadn't changed his mind.

He never would. He'd seen too much, thanks to his father.

There were no *emotions* involved in desiring Marissa Warren. Just some unexplained stupidity. 'We're done here. Let's put you into a taxi so you can get home. Unless you drove to work?' He removed the steno pad and pencil from her grip, pushed them into his briefcase on the table and took her elbow to help her up. A simple courtesy, nothing more.

'I should type the notes while they're fresh. No, I didn't drive. I hire a Mini from a neighbour when I go to Milberry to see Mum and Dad. It's heaps cheaper than owning my own car and I don't often need to drive.' The words stopped abruptly as she came fully to her feet and swayed.

'Marissa? Are you okay?' He pushed her chair

out of the way with his thigh and caught her beneath both elbows even as he registered the personal snippets about her. Registered and wanted to know more, and cursed himself for his curiosity.

'Sorry.' She caught her breath. 'I feel a bit light-headed.' Her body sagged into his hold. For a moment her forehead rested against his chest and all that curly hair was there beneath his chin.

It came naturally to curve his body around hers. He simply did it without thinking. She felt good in his arms, smelled sweetly of gardenias and some other floral scent. He wanted to press his face into her hair and against her skin and inhale until he held the scent of her inside him.

Total insanity, and he had no idea where it had come from. It must be too long since he'd taken a woman to his bed. He had focused more and more on work over recent months.

'Take some deep breaths.' The instruction was to Marissa, though he could do with it himself. 'You won't faint on me, will you?'

'No, I just need a minute.' Her breasts brushed his chest as she drew a series of breaths.

His whole body was sensitised, his vaunted

self-control rocked. He wanted to take her there and then, but he also wanted to cup her head in his hand, tenderly brush her hair from her brow.

Why was she faint, anyway? Lack of food? Was she ill?

'I stood up too fast and I shouldn't have had two bottles of drink in a row like that on an empty stomach. I think I gave myself a sugar overload.' Her fingers curled around his forearms.

'You should take better care of yourself.' The admonition skated far too close to a proprietorial concern. 'I shouldn't have had you work so late without food either.'

'It's my responsibility to eat enough.' She muttered something about thighs and coffee tables.

Rick gave in and raised his hand, stroking his fingers over the soft skin of her jaw. Simply to lift her face, he told himself, to search her eyes, see if she had recovered sufficiently.

Long lashes lifted to reveal brown eyes that slowly came into focus and filled with belated acknowledgement of their nearness.

Perhaps it was the late hour, the silence of the room or the many hours of work that had gone before that momentarily shorted out his brain, because he lowered his head, his lips intent on reaching hers, something inside him determined to make a connection.

She took a deep steadying breath and straightened away from him and the welcome he had glimpsed in her eyes was replaced with the rejection he should have instigated within himself.

The sense of loss startled him and his hands dropped away from her more slowly than they should have. None of this made sense. None of his reactions to her. They shouldn't even exist because he'd told himself to shut down any awareness.

'I'm sorry. I'm fine now.' She held out her hand for her notes and pencil. So she could keep working and truly faint?

'I'll keep these for you for tomorrow.' He closed the briefcase and guided her towards the door. He simply wanted to ensure his employee was okay. This had only truly been geared towards that.

Aggravatingly off-kilter, Rick took Marissa straight to street level and left the building at her side.

'Hand this taxi receipt to accounting so they can reimburse you as well,' he instructed as he flagged a taxi forward from the rank. 'Are you able to start at eight tomorrow? I realise that's early and today has exhausted you but, as well as our regular workload, there's a visit scheduled to a petting zoo. An early lunch for business discussions, and then the zoo itself…'

'I saw that in the BlackBerry.' Her chin hiked into the air and her brown eyes flashed. 'I'll be here at a quarter to eight so I can meet with the supervisor and brief one of the early shift temps on the work required in Gordon's office before we do whatever work we can and then leave. You don't need to make any allowances for me.'

Rather than making him feel bad for asking for another long day out of her, her expression of determination went straight to his groin—a reaction he needed as little as all the others. Perhaps he should have remained in the building and done some laps in the top floor swimming pool before he went home. Like a few hundred or so.

'Then thank you for your willingness to put in the hours.' Rick helped her into the taxi. He would *not* respond to her in such a confusing way again. It was intolerable and unacceptable and he was locking it down right now.

Just like your father would?

And he could leave his family life out of it. That had nothing to do with anything.

'I'll see you tomorrow.' He turned his back and strode away, promising himself he would leave all thoughts of her behind him.

'That's great. Keep smiling. You all look wonderful. Your families will love these photos.' Marissa had two cameras dangling from her left arm by their straps and another one in her hands. At her side Rick held three more.

They were at the brand-new Sydney animal petting zoo and their group of Hong Kong businessmen guests were one hundred per cent enchanted. She and Rick snapped pictures as fast as they could.

She'd made a vow to herself last night when she'd stepped into her sensible apartment in an equally sensible building in a suburb not far from her work.

Actually she'd made it online to Grace and Dani, since they were her Blinddatebrides buddies and, as well as enjoying their long-distance friendship, Marissa felt accountable to them for her dating efforts. It was good to make herself accountable so she would do as she should—find a nice, ordinary, no-surprises man to fall in love with.

Which meant she needed to forget all about being ultra aware of the boss—okay, so she hadn't admitted that part to Dani and Grace.

Rick is interestingly older, though, a mature man with lots of layers. Intriguing, complex.

Someone a mature, well-rounded, thirty-year-old woman might find appealing? Not that she was about to become mature. That made her sound positively ancient and, really, she was just beginning her life.

'How are the photos coming?' Though Rick's question was calm and sensible, the expression in his eyes as he glanced at her still held remnants of yesterday evening's interest.

Marissa's pulse fluttered. 'I'm almost done. Every digital camera is different but I think the shots I'm getting will be fine.'

'Good. That's good.' Rick gestured to the businessmen. 'Perhaps a group shot of all of you?'

He made the suggestion in the deep, even tone he'd used when Marissa had stepped into his office suite this morning and found him already immersed in a deluge of paperwork at his desk. A tone that said they were all about business. But his gaze had contradicted that.

The man had probably invented the term 'confusion'. For anyone near him, that was. And she hadn't wanted him to kiss her last night. She'd simply lost her focus for a moment.

'Hold the pose, gentlemen.' She forced a wide smile as she changed cameras again. 'I need another two photos yet.'

Ozzie the koala didn't seem to mind being held and oohed and aahed over. He sat quietly, his keeper at the side looking on. Ozzie looked utterly adorable with his thick fur and blunt nose and fluffy ears, though his claws were sharp and strong, made for climbing the eucalyptus trees he fed from.

Fortunately the koala was tame and well-behaved. If Marissa could tame her hormones around her boss in the same way, that would be helpful. She took a moment and tried not to *think of* Rick's presence close beside her, or the fact that more than simply her chemical composition seemed interested in him.

She had to see him as her boss and nothing else, and with that in mind, she switched her attention to work. 'Here's hoping this visit ends in a successful outcome.'

'The team seemed pleased with our talks. They'll meet with at least two other major companies before they leave Sydney and then there'll be a period of time before they make a decision, but I'm hopeful.' Rick lowered the final camera and turned his gaze to their visitors.

He smiled towards the group. 'That's the last photo.'

Mr Qi spoke quietly to the keeper and then gestured them over. 'We'd like one of our hosts with Ozzie. Miss Warren will hold him, please.'

To refuse in such circumstances would be out of the question. Instead, Marissa pasted a smile on her face and came forward to hand over her share of the cameras. She drew one long uneasy breath as Rick approached her.

His head bent close to hers. 'Are you okay with this? All the animals here are trained to sit placidly.'

'That's not...' She refused to admit the thought that being close to the boss, not the furry animal's manners concerned her. 'I've never held a koala but I'm not worried he'll hurt me. I just hadn't expected them to ask for this.'

'Sometimes we overlook our own tourist attractions,' he murmured and his gaze roved over her. For all the world as though he felt *he'd* overlooked *her*?

Well, she wasn't much to notice today, in any case. She wore a drab navy cardigan buttoned to the neck over a soft white blouse. A long, ordinary, unadorned navy skirt completed the outfit, so there wasn't a whole lot worth looking at.

Covered from neck to calves in the most unappealing outfit she had? And mostly as a deterrent to herself? To help her not to think about her boss? Who, her?

'Keep the cardigan on while you hold him.'

His comment didn't make a lot of sense, but she gave a small nod to indicate her acquiescence before she turned to face their guests.

They all waited expectantly with cameras poised.

'This will be a thrill for me. Thank you for the opportunity.' It cost nothing to be positive, right? At least Rick hadn't realised the real reason for her unease.

That depressing, confusing, annoying, irritating and wholly aggravating thought disappeared when the keeper put the koala into her arms and another feeling altogether swept through her.

Ozzie cuddled into her like a baby, a warm soft weight with one arm draped over hers and his head turned to the side beneath her chin. Her arms closed around his warmth and a wealth of completely unexpected emotions clogged her throat before her thought processes could catch up with her reaction.

For one long aching moment as Rick stepped behind her, put his arm about her shoulders and she looked up into those intense grey eyes, she longed for the completion of a child. A baby to love and nurture, care for and protect, and the feelings that she'd suppressed over recent months—even longer—all tore through her.

She hadn't impulse-bought that baby wool to make socks for herself. A part of her had reached from way deep down inside for something she wanted, had tried to ignore—how could she want such a thing? It was so foolish to long for something that might never happen for her.

It took two to produce a baby—two willing people and a whole lot of thought and commitment and other things. She should only allow herself hopes and dreams and goals that she knew she could achieve. She certainly did not want to have her boss's baby. It would be absolutely beyond the point of ridiculousness to imagine such a thing.

Even so, Rick's eyes locked with hers and

something deep flickered in his expression, something more than curiosity or simply a man noticing a woman.

Maybe he'd read all those thoughts in her face before she'd been able to mask them? Panic threatened until she assured herself he couldn't possibly have done so. She hadn't realised they were even there until they'd hit her so unexpectedly. Why would he realise such things about her?

'All right?' His gaze was steady as he looked at her, and she managed a shaky breath before the tension fell back enough so that their surroundings came into focus again and she felt in control of herself once more.

'Yes, thanks.' She let her fingers stroke over the koala's soft fur, let herself come back together. 'He's unexpectedly light for his size.'

'A wombat would be far heavier to hold—the compact steamroller of Australian wildlife.' Rick's quip helped ease the moment, they both smiled at long last, and then they smiled for the cameras.

When the photo session ended Rick's arm seemed to linger a moment before he dropped it, but he strode purposefully forward and with due ceremony invited the men to enjoy another hour at the zoo. 'I asked the keepers to save a surprise, and we hope you'll enjoy the opportunity to feed some wombats and kangaroos and other animals while you think over our lunch discussion. There'll be coffee and cake waiting at the restaurant for you when you're finished.'

He left them with smiles and bows and swept Marissa away, who had now pulled herself together. That reaction earlier… It was just some crazy thing that had happened.

She removed her cardigan, rolled it into a ball and wiped her hands on it and warily acknowledged that perhaps biological ticking and the Big 3-0 did appear to have somewhat of an association inside her after all. What to do about that was the question.

When they climbed into Rick's big car, she set the cardigan on the floor behind her seat.

'They smell a bit, don't they?' Rick watched Marissa dispose of her cardigan and tried not to think of that moment back there when she'd first taken the koala into her arms and seemed so surprised and devastated, and he'd wanted to hold *her*, just scoop her up and take her somewhere and cuddle and comfort her.

'Yes, Ozzie smelled of eucalyptus and warm furry animal.' She buckled her seat belt and sat very primly in the seat, her back stiff enough to suggest that she didn't want to delve too deeply into her reaction to holding the animal. 'His coat was a little oily. Thanks for the hint to keep my cardigan on.'

She'd seemed empty somehow, and he'd wanted to give her what was missing, but his response had been on an instinctive level he couldn't begin to fathom. Well, it didn't matter anyway because she was his secretary, nothing more, and since that was exactly how he wanted things to be... 'You're welcome.'

He glanced at her. She was dressed conservatively, but the prissy white blouse just made her hair look fluffier and made him think all the more about the curves hidden away beneath the shirt's modest exterior.

So much for his vow not to think about her as an attractive woman after having his arms around her for those brief moments last night.

'You seemed well prepared for the koala experience.' Her voice held a deliberate calm and good cheer. 'Have you—'

'Held one? Yes. Once.' It hadn't left any notable impact on him, unlike watching her experience today.

Perhaps his instincts towards Marissa weren't entirely dissimilar to those he felt towards his sisters and nieces—a certain protectiveness that rose up because his father had failed to be there for them.

Rick tried to stop the thoughts there. Stephen Morgan was a decent enough man.

Except to Darla, and unless any kind of genuine emotional commitment was required of him. Then Stephen simply dropped the ball as he always had.

Rick forced the thoughts aside. There was nothing he could do about any of that, no way to change a man who inherently wouldn't change. No way to know if Rick himself would be as bad or worse than his father in the same circumstances.

'We often take our overseas business contacts places like this.' It didn't matter what he'd felt for Marissa—or thought he'd felt. By choice he wouldn't act on any response to her, and that was as much for her good as anything else. 'They have a good time and happy businesspeople are more inclined to want to make deals. Those deals mean money and building the business.'

He relaxed into this assertion. It felt comfortable. Familiar. Safe.

When Marissa turned her head to face him, her gaze was curiously flat. 'You're a corporate high-flyer and success means everything to you. I understand.'

She made it sound abhorrent. Why? And success wasn't *everything* to him.

No? That's not what you've been telling yourself and the world for a very long time now.

He did not need to suggest she got to know him better to see other facets of him—all the facets of him. Instead, he agreed with her. 'Success *is* very important to me. You're quite right.'

CHAPTER FIVE

MARISSA hadn't meant to offend Rick. Surely she hadn't? And he *was* a great deal like Michael Unsworth, only more so. She didn't hold that against him, but she had the right to protect herself by remembering the fact.

She didn't want to think about Michael. It was best if she didn't think about *Rick* in any light other than as her employer. And she certainly didn't want to dwell on that hormonal whammy that had hit her back at the petting zoo.

If she wanted something to cuddle, she probably needed a kitten or something.

Do you hear me, hormones and non-existent clock? This is my *destiny and I choose what I want and need and don't need.*

She refused to be dictated to on the topic by any internal systems. With that thought in mind, she worked hard for the rest of the day, and cursed the stubborn part of her that insisted on admiring Rick's business acumen as she came to see more and more of it in play. Couldn't she ignore that at least?

Maybe she should simply admit it. She liked his drive and determination. With a frown, she shoved another file away in the room dedicated to that purpose just off their suite's reception room.

More files were slapped home. Not because she was fed up with herself. She was simply being efficient.

Yes. Sure. That was the truth of it. A pity she didn't seem capable of the same single-mindedness when it came to finding Mr Right through Blinddatebrides.com. She'd yet to initiate any kind of invitation to a man, had cancelled that second drink yesterday, and hadn't looked at those ten profiles as she'd told herself she would. She'd been bored by all the candidates she'd met so far.

Grace had dated a man straight up on joining the site, even if she had panicked about it at the time.

Dani remained tight-lipped so far about dates but she sure seemed to have her head together about the whole process, right down to the site's efficiency and how it all worked. Why couldn't Marissa follow *her* plan there, and stop fixating on the boss?

Marissa had logged on in her tea break, anyway. It wasn't her fault she'd run out of time before she could do more than read some of the contact messages.

Shove, shuffle, push.

'I'll be on the top level for the next hour.' Rick spoke from the doorway in a tone that didn't reveal even the smallest amount of any kind of sensual anticipation he surely should feel in the face of yet another 'meeting' with the mysterious Julia, who seemed to have a place reserved for her almost daily in his diary.

That was something Marissa had discovered today as she'd scanned ahead further in the BlackBerry to try to gauge the kind of workload they might have ahead of them.

Well, good on him for seeing this Julia. With such a knowledge foremost in her thoughts, Marissa simply wouldn't look at him as an available man, which was *all to the good*.

It was just as well the woman didn't mind being slotted in like a visit to the dentist or a board meeting or teleconference, though.

Marissa shoved two more files away and forced herself to face him. 'You won't mind if I take a short break myself? I'll just talk on the

Internet with friends. There's nothing in the diary—'

Marissa broke off a little uneasily, but Rick wasn't to know those friends were on an Internet dating site with her. Not that she cared who knew she had a subscription to a dating website. She could do what she liked. It was her life and just because she hadn't even told her parents she'd joined Blinddatebrides.com didn't mean she felt uncomfortable about it or anything.

Grace and Dani knew she wanted to find a nice man. Marissa had been very open with them really.

Her online friends were signed up to the dating site, of course, so Marissa hadn't exactly been exposing deep secrets by admitting she wanted to meet some men. And she hadn't told Grace and Dani everything about herself by any means. She certainly hadn't told them her plan to clinically vet those men until she found one she was prepared to fall in love with.

Well, that was her business, and it mightn't even happen and her vetting ideas made a lot of sense.

'Please do take a break.' Rick turned. 'I sought you out to suggest that.'

A moment later, after delivering that piece of thoughtfulness, he was gone.

Marissa appreciated the reprieve from close contact with him. That was what made her feel all mushy and approving, not only his consideration for her. She told herself this as she logged onto Blinddatebrides.com and scrolled through the messages she'd skimmed earlier. This time she made herself read them and follow through to look at profiles.

And she set her fingers to the keyboard and replied that she would be delighted—*delighted*—to arrange something with Tony, 32, computer software. Perhaps lunch tomorrow?

Marissa got off the site without checking for instant messages from Grace or Dani. She wasn't avoiding them. She just felt guilty about giving herself the time when she should be working, even if Rick was on the top floor of the building with Julia doing she didn't want to think about what.

When the fax machine made its warming-up sound, Marissa left her desk with a rather desperate alacrity. She'd struggled to concentrate on her typing despite her determination to plough through as much work as possible before Rick got back.

She snatched up the first page of the fax and

skimmed it, and then read it more carefully while two more pages emerged from the machine. If the large 'urgent' stamp on the top of the first page hadn't been clue enough, the contents were, drat it all to pieces. She'd hoped for something to distract her thoughts, but not this way.

'I'll ring his mobile phone and tell him he needs to get back here. It's not my problem there's an emergency and I'll be interrupting…whatever.' She walked to her desk and pressed the speed dial for his mobile number, only to return the phone to its cradle when the thing rang from on top of his desk in the next room.

What now? Try another department head? Which one? The contents of the fax covered material from all the departments.

'Right, so there's no choice. It's marked for his attention specifically, and it's urgent.' Marissa snatched the door key from her purse and pushed it into her pocket. If she could have thought of any other way to handle this, she'd have taken it.

The trip to the top level went by far too fast. She'd never been up here before. There seemed to be a large atrium surrounded by rooms behind closed doors.

Rick's workaday lair? A place to come when he wanted privacy without leaving the building?

She'd crossed half the cavernous expanse of tiled floor flanked with tall banks of potted ornamental trees, the fax clutched in a death grip in her hand, before she realised the sounds of splashing weren't from an indoor fountain.

Marissa's gaze lifted and the view in front of her cleared just in time for her to see strong arms lift a little girl out of the water and pass her to a dark-haired woman who stood beside…a swimming pool.

Rick was in the pool, his wide shoulders and thick arms exposed and water dripping from his face and down his chest.

Just the right amount of dark hair there.

What on earth is going on here?

Child. Woman. Rick in the pool and not a sensual indicator to be detected in the room.

And finally this thought:

That's what the swimming roster that circulates by email means, the slots for before work each day.

She'd only seen the email twice, and had thought the staff took turns booking some *other* swimming facilities.

Marissa's steps faltered to a stop.

'Thank you, Unca Rick.' The little girl waited impatiently while the woman removed her flotation devices, only to immediately lean fearlessly over the edge of the pool, arms extended, to the man who was Marissa's boss—in a very different guise right now.

He was a specimen of male beauty and Marissa couldn't take her gaze from him. The child would have tumbled back in if the woman hadn't held onto her arm. If Rick hadn't immediately caught her by the tiny waist. Big gentle hands keeping her from harm.

The little girl planted a kiss on Rick's cheek and his arms came around her, his hands gently patting her back before he set her on her feet again beside the pool.

'You're welcome.' Oh, the soft deepness of his voice.

Marissa's abdomen clenched in a reaction she wholly did not want to admit was happening. She hadn't joined Blinddatebrides.com to find Mr Virile and Able to Produce Strong Children, nor Mr Gentle and Sweet With Said Children. She certainly wasn't looking for those traits in the man before her.

'The next time *you'll* put your head all the way under the water, okay, Julia?' His smile was gentle, encouraging and, to Marissa, quite devastating. 'Fishes do that all the time.'

Julia…

The woman smiled and turned her head and the likeness between all three of them clicked it all fully into place.

This child was Julia—a sweet little girl about four or five years old with a shock of dark hair flattened wet against the back of her head and still dry in the front. The woman beside the pool was Rick's sister. The entire scene was so far removed from what Marissa had expected, she couldn't seem to find her breath or get her legs to move.

Or perhaps that was simply the impact of so much raw sensual appeal concentrated in the man in front of her, and the crazy twisting of reactions inside her.

And Rick wasn't involved.

Now she thought about it, hadn't Gordon said when she'd first started here that Rick was a solitary man and seemed to keep his dating lowkey and…transitory?

And hello, that wouldn't exactly make him a candidate for a relationship. Plus Marissa didn't want to have one with him. He might be in a swimming pool, but the term 'corporate shark' still meant more than a boss doing laps in chlorine-scented water.

Oh, but he hadn't looked like a boss or a shark when he'd held his niece so tenderly in his arms. Marissa clenched her teeth because she *was not going down this track and that was that!*

Maybe she made a sound because Rick's head turned and his expression closed as though she'd caught him at something he hadn't wanted her to see.

Why would he feel that way about giving a swimming lesson to his niece? Not only that, but surely he'd guessed what Marissa thought about 'Julia' and yet he hadn't said a word.

'I'm sorry for barging in.' Sorry and quite annoyed by his hidden depths, whether that made her unreasonable or not. 'I have an urgent fax and I thought—' She'd thought he'd be behind one of those closed doors beyond the pool with a lover. 'Er…I didn't realise there was a swimming pool up here.'

'It's not a problem. We've taken enough of Rick's time away from his work anyway.' The woman smiled as she wrapped her daughter in a towel and gathered her into her arms. 'I'm Faith, by the way. Rick's youngest sister.'

'Marissa.' She sought the comfortable communication skills that should have flowed naturally. 'Marissa Warren. I'm filling in while Rick's secretary, Tom, is on sick leave.'

'Ah, I see. For a while?' The other woman glanced at Rick and her eyes seemed to gleam. 'That should make for an interesting change.'

'It's not for all that long.' Rick cleared his throat. 'Didn't you say you needed to be going, Faith?'

His sister's mouth softened. 'Yes. There's a chance we might get a call from Russell tonight if things with his unit go as planned. I don't want to miss that. I asked Mum and Dad if they'd like to come over, speak with him and then watch you-know-who while I finish the call. The deployments are hard and he doesn't have his parents around, but Mum and Dad were too busy.'

Something in Rick's face seemed to tighten with… sadness? Some kind of regret for his sister? A measure of long-standing anger? 'What time? Do you want me to phone conference in from the office?'

'No, that's okay.' Faith lifted her daughter

higher into her arms. 'Julia and I will be fine on our own but I appreciate the offer.'

They left after that and Marissa faced the company's boss where he stood in the water. No tattoo on the right biceps. Just muscles that seemed to invite the stroke of questing fingers. Marissa wanted to stay annoyed at him for concealing the truth about Julia from her. Instead, she could only see his kindness to his sister and niece, meshed with the appeal of a great deal of male sensuality.

Somehow *this* Rick was even deeper and more difficult to try to ignore. 'Your niece and sister seem lovely. It's…er…it's kind of you to give the little girl swimming lessons.'

'I'm a skilled diver and for some reason Julia feels safer in the water with a man.' His closed expression warned her off the topic, yet families were all about being there for each other, right?

Why would he mind her knowing he'd been there for his sister and niece?

Before she could consider possible answers, he climbed from the pool. In the brief time it took him to walk to the nearby lounger, snatch up a towel and wrap it around his hips, her concentration fled completely.

'I always try to swim here every day anyway.' His gaze swept, heavy-lidded and resistantly aware, over her. 'For the exercise.'

'You look very fit. Exceptionally fit, really. Quite muscularly fit.' Heat washed over her from her toes to the top of her head as she acknowledged that saying so might not have been particularly prudent. And why was he looking at her that way? He was the half-naked one.

Board shorts and a towel. The man is perfectly adequately covered. This was quite true. The problem was that the board shorts had clung, hadn't they? And the towel still left a lot of skin on display. His waist was trim and his shoulders were stunning.

'Your hair wasn't wet yesterday.' The blurted words were an accusation, as though, if his hair had been wet and she'd worked out he'd been swimming, she would have felt more prepared for the sight of him this way. 'And you didn't smell like chlorine. I have a really good nose for that sort of thing.'

'Today's the first day Julia's allowed me to put my head under the water, and I shower afterwards.' His hair fell in a dripping mass over one side of his forehead and was pushed back from the other.

Spiked lashes blinked away the droplets of water that clung to them. 'I want her to like swimming so I have to accommodate her fears. With her father away, she needs someone…'

'I…er…it must be difficult for your sister, having a husband in the armed forces and unable to do the daddy things at times.' Did the words even make sense? How could she concentrate, with every ounce of her so aware of the sight of him this way?

Not only that, but her hormones insisted on pointing out that Rick had seemed quite appealing indeed in the daddy role. Well, uncle, but it was the same general kind of thing.

Not really.

Yes, really.

She had to get over this idea of wanting a baby!

She had *not* thought that in association with Rick, anyway. She'd merely had a brief moment of considering how, in a bygone time, as in at *the dawn of time*, women may have reacted to strong men by wanting to…um…mate with them.

Which Marissa did not want to do—at all, whatsoever—with her boss.

It seemed expedient to get out of here. But

she couldn't quite recall how to bring that about. 'Um…well…'

'Yes?' Rick's gaze locked with Marissa's. He felt worked up and overwrought for no reason he could explain. Other than to name the reason 'Marissa' or, at the least, 'his reaction to Marissa'. That was something he didn't want to do.

Her fingers tightened around the papers in her hands. 'The fax.'

'Let me see what it says.' He took the pages from her, careful not to touch her. Bent his head to read while she finally looked everywhere but at him.

The knowledge of that belated restraint absurdly made him want her all the more. 'I'll need the files on this from the Civil Engineering department. Go straight there, will you? See if you can catch someone before they close for the day but tell him or her they don't need to hang around. This is something I'll have to address myself.'

'I'll go right now.' With relief evident in every line of her body and expression on her face, Marissa took the fax, wheeled about and escaped with it.

Rick watched her go. She seemed more than glad to get away from him now. Which was, of course, exactly as he wanted things to be…

CHAPTER SIX

From: Englishcrumpet
Just let Tony down gently.

From: Sanfrandani
Better to tell the man so he knows where he stands.

From: Kangagirl
I know you're both right. I don't want to hurt his feelings, that's all. Tony is a really nice guy. Maybe I shouldn't have met with him twice so close together. We had lunch the day after I found my boss giving his niece a swimming lesson on the top floor of our work building, and then we had dinner tonight. If I'd given myself more time between…

From: Englishcrumpet

Do you really think seeing Tony this Saturday or next would have made any difference? What exactly did you say was wrong with him, anyway?

From: Sanfrandani
No spark, wasn't it?

From: Kangagirl
Yes, and that's enough about me and my evening. Tell me about your dating efforts.

'This is a very tall building.' The words passed through Marissa's lips despite herself as they travelled up the outside of the building-in-progress in a cage lift.

It was Monday morning. She'd survived the disappointment of yet again finding 'no spark' during that second date with Tony, had also survived an entire week of working for Rick Morgan.

Had survived by the skin of her self-control, actually, and, really scarily tall buildings should be the least of her concerns.

For the real challenge, try genuinely not noticing the boss who'd taken her to the scary tall building in the first place, rather than merely pretending not to notice him. He superimposed himself on the Blinddatebrides men's profile pictures when she viewed them, took over her brain space during her dating efforts. Marissa felt a spark all right—towards completely the wrong man!

Her fingers tightened their death grip on the handrail inside the cage. 'And the lift is very fast.'

Dizzyingly so now she'd made the mistake of watching things whizz past. She'd thought that might save her from looking at Rick.

'We're quite secure, despite the fact you can see everything around you.' He took her elbow to help her off as the lift stopped. Held on while she came to terms with the height. Held on and her skin tingled while his expression deepened because of their nearness. 'Don't worry.' His voice seemed to come from deep in his chest as he placed his body between hers and the outside of the construction so she only saw him. 'I've got you. I won't let anything happen to you.'

She'd been half okay until he said that. Now she had to add chivalry to his list of attributes.

'Thank you, but I'm sure I'll be quite fine now.' She forced herself to step away from him, did her best to ignore the ache that doing so left behind.

Rick's hand dropped slowly to his side as though he too hadn't been ready to lose that contact.

Had touching her jolted him the same way? The answer was in the lock of his muscles, the tightness of his jaw and the way his lids lowered as his gaze drifted from her eyes to her mouth.

Then suddenly he turned to greet the site manager and the construction boss led them over every inch of the building.

Marissa composed herself and gave the tour her determined attention. This was a genuine meeting, the kind that should happen, not the sort where a man went on about turning a bridge into something completely made-over when that simply wasn't possible.

She took pages of notes of specifications that Rick would expect her to incorporate when he worked on his department memos after the visit and decided she was okay with this. She had it all under control now. All she needed to do was keep her attention on her work, not look at her boss any more than she had to and not think about him at all.

Yes. And that worked really well when they were in constant communication at point blank range, didn't it?

'Overall, the project looks good at this stage.' Rick nodded his approval as they finished their discussion at ground level almost an hour later.

'I'm happy enough with things so far.' The site boss pushed his hard hat back off his head. 'But we have two more days of work, maximum, before we need that shipment of materials from the Melbourne supplier. If we don't get it by then, we're stalled and that's going to cost us in time and wages.'

'And you think the reason for the delay is related to underlying union issues at their end?' Rick nodded. 'Let me look into this. I'll see if I can get things moving for you. Do you have a copy of the order?'

'Right here.' The site boss removed it from his clipboard.

Rick took it, glanced at it and passed it to Marissa. 'At least you won't have to note all this down.'

Their fingers brushed. His words brushed across her senses at the same time. Just words, but his gaze searched her face, took her in as though he didn't realise he was doing it. As though he couldn't stop himself from doing it.

'I hope we can get back to the office soon.' She needed the security of her desk and at least some semblance of routine. She needed Tom to get better fast and come back to work so she could hide in Gordon's office.

More than that, she needed to stamp the words 'dating website' on her forehead so she remembered what she was supposed to be doing.

Not *supposed* to. *Wanted* to. *Must do. Was doing!* 'So I can get to work on this transcribing.'

They made their way back to work with Rick dictating on the way. Once at the office, Marissa worked on his department memos and, because they were so pushed for time, they ate lunch at their desks. The busy afternoon that followed shouldn't have allowed time to feel anything but the strain of hours of hard work, and yet she felt a great deal of *other* strain.

Marissa wished that strain away as she made yet another phone call for her boss. 'This is Marissa Warren. I'm filling in as Rick Morgan's secretary and need you to supply me with a list of names of all the people who've worked on the Chartrel project.' She clasped the phone against her ear and smelled Rick's scent on it from when he'd taken a call at her desk minutes earlier.

Marissa closed her eyes and inhaled before she could stop herself. When she lifted her lids again, Rick's gaze rested on her from the other room, deep grey eyes honed on her.

She forced her attention back to her work, buried herself in it. Maybe she should never emerge again. That might fix things. When Rick came to her desk an hour later, she knew it hadn't fixed anything at all.

'I need you to take these to the departments personally, Marissa.' He held out several signed memos. 'I know we're busy, but I want you to wait for their responses.'

'All right.' She agreed without hesitation. Eager to please him. No. She wasn't overly compliant or willing to go the extra mile. She certainly didn't think they were equals in this and would both be rewarded at the end. The roles were clear. Hers and his. This wasn't the same as the past.

Rick wasn't using her to try to make himself look bigger or better.

Maybe not, but he was still using her in his

own way. He'd swept her into working for him without giving her a choice.

Your employment contract states: 'and other duties as required'. He didn't ask you to do anything you're not obliged to do.

Fine. The man had every right to commandeer her. He was still too similar to Michael—all business orientation and focused on his work goals. Marissa held the thought up like a shield, and added another. She wanted to find a safe man, an ordinary man, and yes, okay, maybe she did want to get married and fulfil the promise of the Blinddatebrides.com website.

She *was* almost thirty. Surely a desire for genuine commitment was acceptable at that age? Her mother had been married a decade by then, with a child—what if Marissa could only have one baby, like Mum had?

Didn't it make sense that Marissa might be thinking of getting started on that? That was nothing more than a logistics thing.

She wheeled about. 'When I get back, I'll do something about the explosion out here that was once my…that is…Tom's desk.'

Not her desk.

Tom's desk.

Tom's chair.

She was keeping it all warm for *Tom* and nothing more. On this fortifying reminder, she left. Graciously and calmly, as befitted someone totally in control of her life, her hopes, her dreams and herself.

By the middle of the afternoon it was raining—a drenching fall that obscured the skyline and turned the water in the harbour choppy. Marissa stared at the dismal view before she turned back to the photocopier.

'Deep breath,' she muttered. This was an irritation, after all, not a major problem. She eased open the three side doors on the machine, the one at the back, and pulled out both paper drawers and hit the spring catch on the feed cover so she could see in there as well.

Paper jams happened and, yes, there would now be pages missing from the report and she'd have to figure out what she'd lost, but that was *fine*.

The printer had needed a new ink cartridge an hour ago. One of the computer applications had quit mid-keystroke and she'd lost a few minutes of work. The phone continued to ring hot and there'd been more people from other departments through the door today than in the entirety of last week. She had enough typing sitting on her desk to take her the rest of the day by itself.

Rick was also busy. He was deep in phone talks about some crisis or another right now and it was clear from the content of the several tapes he'd asked her to work on 'urgently' that he was handling the equivalent of photocopier breakdown times about a thousand from *his* desk.

The corporate shark was doing his thing with a great deal of style today, controlling his world, working through problems, making it all come together despite the difficulties and…thriving on it and being cheerful about it as he went along. Marissa did not find this at all stimulating, and it did not show her a different side of her boss, making it exponentially more difficult for her to keep viewing him as a corporate danger zone.

'Let's go. We're finished with this for today.' The day had felt interminable to Rick. From that trip up the building construction, when he'd wanted to protect Marissa, keep her safe, never let anything happen to her, through the rainy afternoon and on into this evening, Rick had struggled with his attraction to her.

She was amazing, the way she got down to work without a word of complaint, no matter what was thrown at her. And he…found that too appealing about her.

Maybe that explained this current madness, because not only was he determined to take her out of the office and feed her, he had no intention of letting her refuse. He took her bag from the desk drawer and pressed it into her hands, and drew her out of her chair.

Well, it was no big deal. Marissa deserved a reward for working so hard. As her boss, he wanted to give her that reward. He'd done the same for Tom countless times.

But this wasn't Tom and, the moment Rick touched Marissa, desire buzzed through his system and threatened to overwhelm him. Well, he would control that desire by the force of his will—maybe he needed to show himself he could do that.

'Wait. What are you doing? I have work up on the computer and I'm nowhere near finished.' She dug her shoes into the carpet, her eyes wide and startled as surprise and uncertainty and the same fire he fought in his bloodstream all bloomed in her gaze.

'We're going to eat and then go to our respective homes to get some rest.' That sounded suitably businesslike. A pity he ruined it by adding, 'The office can wait until tomorrow.'

Not only had he not intended to downplay the importance of his work, but his voice had mellowed as his gaze roved over her, over the hair sticking out from the times she'd whipped the transcription headset on and off, and bent over the photocopier cursing.

She had trousers on today. Pale tan trousers and a black cashmere top that hugged her curves, and soft leather lace-up shoes she hadn't needed to change for their fieldwork.

Though the clothing screamed 'comfortable' and 'sensible' it also lovingly displayed every curve. He'd believed himself beyond reacting to those curves now.

Fooled yourself, you mean.

Well, it was too late to back out of this dinner now. Instead, he scooped everything on her desk into the tray and locked it away while she gasped. Then he shut down her computer and hustled her to the door.

'We're eating.' As colleagues. An hour in her company outside of working hours might take care of his inexplicable interest in her in any case. What did he know of her, after all, personally? She might bore him to tears. He might do the same to her. 'Don't argue. There are shadows under your eyes. And if there's too much work for you we'll farm some out to the general staff.'

This was not an option that had ever occurred to him before. That it did now shocked him into a silence that lasted the entire ride in the lift to the underground parking area.

As he helped her into his big car, she spoke.

'I'm not overwhelmed by the workload and it's kind of you to want to feed me but I assure you I'm not faint or anything.' She turned her head to face him. 'I've taken care to eat snacks regularly since that incident the first day.'

'I know.' He'd been watching, had checked on her though she wouldn't have realised he was doing it. And, because that knowledge of himself made him feel exposed, he reiterated, 'This is not a kindness. It's a reward for efforts rendered, for both of us, that's all. And I'm pleased to hear it about the workload because, in truth, I don't really like the idea of handing work out of my office.'

They passed the rest of the trip in silence. He figured it was just as well since the words coming out of his mouth didn't seem to be much under his control.

When they arrived at the restaurant, Rick settled Marissa at the table in the same way he seemed to manage everything. With care and courtesy and without any hint of being the user and taker Michael Unsworth was.

'Thank you.' How could Marissa keep up her shield against her boss when he behaved this way? Right now she didn't want to, and that was a dangerous attitude. 'I've finally managed to take a breath for the first time today. I guess…I'm glad you thought of this, of us catching a quick meal on the way home.'

Marissa toyed with her water glass and tried not to think how nice it *was* to be seated opposite Rick in the tiny restaurant tucked away in a side street only about a ten minute drive from his offices.

Bilbie's @ Eighty-Eight sported just a handful of dining tables, spaced far apart and lit individually with a fat red candle on a chipped saucer in the centre of each.

Rain stung the darkened windows and the street lights and car headlights blurred out there, but inside all was quiet and calm.

Well, except for the tension she felt as she finally lifted her gaze and looked into Rick's eyes. Because it was a tension that had nothing to do with residual work stresses, that had an intimacy to it that just wouldn't seem to leave them.

Despite Rick's assertion this was nothing more than a reward for hard work. Despite her need to be attracted to someone other than him.

The latter wasn't working out very well right now.

So why hadn't she declined this meal with him?

Good manners. It might have seemed churlish if she'd refused.

Sure, Marissa. That's what it is.

Rick tore a piece of dense crusty bread from the loaf and dipped it in the herbed dressing and held it out to her. 'It would take as long for you to go home and prepare something for your dinner.'

'Thank you. I didn't realise what I was missing. Here. With this restaurant. It's…a nice setting. You know, for colleagues to visit briefly on a one-off basis. I don't find it romantic at all. I'm sure you don't either. Overall, I'd say the place is homely.' She popped the bread in her mouth before she could say anything else.

The taste and texture of the food enticed a soft sigh from her. The sight of his intent expression as he watched her did the same again. 'The bread…the…er…the bread is delicious.'

'The décor could do with a facelift.' In the candlelight the grey of his eyes darkened as his gaze focused on her. His lashes cast shadows over the strong slash of his cheeks. 'I don't particularly like the colour red either. I prefer autumn tones, like your—' He frowned. 'Like the season.'

Like her hair and the clothing she chose to wear most often? Marissa felt warmed despite herself.

Was she so foolish that she couldn't avoid falling for this kind of man again? For her ex-fiancé's kind of man? Because Rick *was* corporate to the core. He wouldn't care about building a family or doing any of the things she wanted…

'Feta on warm salad.' A waiter deposited the entrées and whisked a bottle of white wine forward, poured and left the rest of the bottle on the table. Disappeared again.

Rick drew a deep breath. 'Eat.' He gestured to the food, lifted his fork and seemed determined to back the tension off. Back it right off and keep it backed off.

Marissa wanted that too. To assist in that endeavour, she said a little desperately, 'You said you're a skilled diver. Is that something you've done for long?'

Small talk. Surely if she smothered them in small talk it would have the desired effect?

'I started diving in my twenties after my sister Darla… For leisure.' He sipped his wine and something in his face seemed to close up. 'I've dived coastal reefs and other places but nowadays I mostly work locally on some endangered species projects.'

'Your niece really is in good hands with her swimming lessons, then.' A flash of that day, of him bare-chested and off-centre as he'd made up excuses for those swimming lessons, did something warm and tingly to her insides. It softened her emotions and made it difficult to remember him as the high-flying boss, a man very much out of her emotional league.

'Your family—'

'I'd rather hear about you.' He didn't bark the words, but the closed door was clear just the same. 'About your interests. We probably don't have a lot in common.'

No. They probably didn't, and she should appreciate that he wanted them both to accept that.

Rick let his gaze slide to his hands for a moment as he asked, 'So. What are your hobbies?'

What hadn't she tried might be easier to answer. But here was her chance to bore him rigid.

Marissa realised they'd eaten their way through the food and she hadn't even noticed. Well, she was focused now.

'I've tried motorcycle riding. I was eighteen and had a boyfriend at the Milberry further education college that year. He had tattoos and really long hair.' Was that enough boredom factor? 'I also tried my hand as a jillaroo on an outback station for twelve months but I guess that's a career, not a hobby. Does it count as a hobby if you just tested it out to see how it fit?'

She'd missed her parents a lot during that twelve months. And she was fighting to try to be boring. This wasn't supposed to be a cheerful reminiscence session.

His eyes gleamed with interest that he probably didn't want to feel either. 'I can't imagine you roping calves or whatever girl station hands do.'

Maybe if she went on some more he'd reach that stage of boredom they both wanted.

'I *can* ride a horse, though I'd only had pony

club lessons before I went outback.' Her parents had found the money to give her those childhood lessons. They'd been filled with pride the first time she'd taken her little borrowed pony once around the walking ring all by herself. 'The jillaroo thing didn't really work out. I found I didn't like dust and big open spaces all that much.'

Instead of questioning her lack of intrepidity or yawning, he laughed. A deep, rich sound that rippled over her skin and made her catch her breath, and made him look years younger even as his laugh faded abruptly.

Their main courses arrived. Fillet of sole for her on a bed of spiced lentil mash, salmon steak for him with green beans and wild rice.

Marissa though he might leave the discussion there, or change the topic. Or simply let the silence grow as its own demonstration of his complete lack of interest in the minutiae of her life.

Instead, he caught her glance again and said, almost desperately, 'What else have you done with your time?'

'I went through a craft phase that lasted several years.' Surely he would find that very ordinary. She sipped her wine and a part of her registered the wonderful fruity tartness against her tongue before she went on. 'I crocheted a throw rug, made one patchwork quilt—a very small one. Tried out bag beading and made a tissue box cover, created my own calendar out of photos.'

Bought baby wool and hid it in the bottom drawer of my dresser, even though I know it's there and there's a part of me that wants to get it out and buy a knitting pattern for tiny little booties and work out how to make them.

Why did she have to feel this way? Why did she suddenly want all these things with an ever-increasing fierceness? Was it just because she was soon to turn thirty? Well, whatever the reason, it was highly inconvenient and she wished she didn't feel this way, and it was really not conducive to her peace of mind to have such thoughts in Rick's presence!

'And you've made a laminated desk cover of cartoons. I glanced at some of them. You've gathered some good material.' Though his words were bland, the look in his eyes was anything but.

'I've tried out a lot of different things. I'm not like that about work, though,' she hastened to add. 'I'm perfectly happy at Morgan's and hope to stay with the company for a very long time.'

'You've worked with us about six months, haven't you?' As easily as the conversation had rambled through her hobbies, it shifted to ground she didn't want to visit. 'What about before that? There's a stretch of time between those early things and now.' And now he looked interested in quite a different way.

Marissa tried not to let her body stiffen but she so didn't want to answer his question. She shouldn't have let the conversation head in this direction at all. 'I worked as a secretary in marketing for a number of years before…before I moved into my lovely position working for Gordon. I also like my apartment here better than the old one.'

There were no memories of her stupidity within its walls. Michael had never lived with her, but he'd spent time in her home.

Well, a complete break had been in order, and why was she thinking about that when she'd deliberately pushed it out of her mind straight after it had happened? Had learned the lesson and moved right along.

Had she? Or was she defensive on more than one front and trying to patch over the problems by finding a special man she could hand-pick at her own discretion? That question rose up just to add something else to her broodiness and worries about ageing, as if they weren't big enough problems by themselves.

Her mouth tightened. 'And Morgan's is a great company to work for. Anyway, you don't want to hear that boring stuff about me.' She waved a hand.

'Maybe I do.' His intent gaze questioned her. 'What made you leave your previous position? Was it a career choice or something more personal?'

She tightened her lips and shook her head, forcing a soft laugh from between teeth inclined to clench together. 'It was time for a change of pace for me, that's all. Now it's your turn. Have you ever learned to crochet or knit, or maybe taken cooking lessons?' Maybe those questions would shut him down?

'Funny. No. None of those.' For a moment it seemed he would pursue the topic of her career choices but in the end he let it go and moved on. 'I'm not much of a cook, to be honest.' And then he said, 'My eldest niece is taking lessons. She's sixteen and a combination of teenage angst one minute and little girl vulnerability the next. Darla, my other sister, is a good mother to her. The best.'

And then he speared a piece of bean with his fork and chewed it and fell silent and stayed that way until the meal ended.

Eventually he lifted the wine bottle. 'Another glass?'

'No, thank you. I've had enough.' She wished she could blame the wine for the slow slide away of the barriers she needed to keep in place in his company.

Instead of controlling her attraction, she longed to ask more about his family, despite his tendency to guard any words about them.

'Coffee, then.' Rick signalled and a waiter magically appeared.

She drew a breath. 'Yes, coffee would be nice.' Maybe that would sober her thoughts, though she'd had very little to drink.

The beverages arrived. His gaze narrowed on her. 'You're lost in thought.'

Not thoughts he'd want to know. She forced a smile. 'I *should* be thinking. About work tomorrow.' About the fact that they were boss and employee and this evening had been a reward to her as his employee. Nothing more. 'The rain seems to have stopped.'

'Yes.' He turned his gaze to the windows,

almost as though he knew she needed a reprieve from his attention.

They finished their drinks in silence.

'I'll take you home.' He placed some notes inside the leather account folder and got to his feet.

Outside the restaurant, he ushered her into his car and waited for her address. When she gave it, he put the car into motion. She wanted to make easy conversation and lighten the mood but no words would come. Then they were outside her apartment building and she turned to face him.

'Thank you for feeding me dinner.' *Will you kiss me goodnight? Do I want you to?* 'It wasn't necessary.' And she mustn't want any such thing. Naturally *he* wouldn't want it!

'Your cheeks are flushed. Even in this poor light I can see.' He murmured the words as though he couldn't stop them. 'It's like watching roses bloom. I took you to dinner to prove we have nothing in common but work, and yet...' He threw his door open, climbed out of the vehicle.

He did want her still. Despite everything.

The warmth in Marissa's cheeks doubled and her heart rate kicked into overdrive, even as she sought some other explanation for her conclusion. It *had to be* the wine.

She mustn't be attracted to him, or to his layers. Yet she struggled to remember all the valid reasons why not.

His hand went to the small of her back to lead her inside. 'Ready?'

CHAPTER SEVEN

'WELL, here we are, right at my door,' Marissa babbled as she opened said door, and then appalled herself by adding, 'Would you care to—?'

'For a moment.' He stepped in after her, and then there they were, facing each other in her small living room.

Her fourth floor apartment was functional and neat. A lamp glowed from a corner table. She flicked a switch on the wall and the room came fully into focus—the lounge suite in a dark chocolate colour with a crushed velvet finish, her crocheted throw rug folded neatly at one end.

Prints on the walls and a kitchen cluttered full of gaily coloured canisters and racks of spices completed the picture. 'It's nothing special,' she said, 'but I've tried to make it a home.'

'You succeeded.' His gaze went to the lounge and returned to her face, and a desire he had fought—they had both fought—burned in his eyes.

'Well, thank you again.' She shifted beside him. Wanted him to stay. Forced herself not to offer coffee, late night TV, late night Marissa…

'Goodnight. I shouldn't have come in.' His gaze tracked through her home again.

'Yes. Goodnight. You should…go.'

The muscle of his upper arm brushed the curve of her shoulder as he turned. He made a choked sound and his fingers grasped her wrist.

'We mustn't—' But she lifted her head as his lowered and then his mouth was on hers.

He tasted of coffee and wine and Rick—a wonderful, fulfilling taste that she lost herself in. So totally lost herself…

Rick's stomach muscles clenched as he fought the urge—almost the *need*—to crush Marissa close. He didn't *need*. He made choices.

Like this one? What was he doing?

Marissa made a soft sound in her throat and her hand lifted to his biceps, and then his shoulder, over his shirt. He wanted her hand on his skin. Somewhere. Anywhere. To warm him…

When she finally stroked her fingers over the cord of his neck and up to the edge of his jaw, he pressed in to her touch. As though he couldn't survive without it. The feeling was shocking, almost unmanning, and yet still he kissed her, pressed nearer, kept going.

Rick caught her hand as it dropped away from his face. Caught it between their bodies with his and held it to his chest. Felt eased somewhere deep inside as he did this.

He meant to control this. It was only desire. It had to be—he could still prove it. Somehow. If he merely kissed her again, tasted her again and then…

The *and then* part didn't happen. Not in the way he intended. Not *Goodbye* and *Glad you enjoyed the dinner* and *That was nothing out of the ordinary.*

Instead, he should ask what the hell he was doing kissing her in the first place.

Even that question couldn't get through. Not with his lips fused to hers, their bodies a breath apart. It should have—it needed to. A part of Rick acknowledged that. He kissed her again anyway. Kissed her and drew her against his chest and wondered if he was stark, staring crazy as his heart thundered and his arms ached to keep her within their clasp.

Marissa didn't know what to do. She'd let this get out of her control and she didn't know how to bring it back. Rick's kiss, his touch, his arms around her all combined not only to swamp her senses but also to overwhelm her in too many other ways.

His hold felt like a haven, his touch what she had needed and waited for. Her emotions were involved in this kiss, and she couldn't let them be. She had to protect herself. He didn't even want to desire her, and she was determined to have no feelings for him. She *didn't* have feelings for him. Right? *Right?*

She gasped and drew sharply back. Her hands dropped from him.

He released her in the same instant, and stared at her as though he couldn't believe what he'd done. As though his actions astounded him. As though he'd *felt* them in the same deep places she had?

Don't fool yourself, Marissa.

His jaw locked tight. 'I showed a weakness of character by doing that. I apologise.' He stepped back from her and the warmth of his eyes returned to a stark, flat grey.

Marissa wanted to take consolation in the fact

that he looked as though he had run a marathon, looked as torn and stunned and taken aback as she felt, but he'd soon recovered his voice, hadn't he? And his self-control. She had to do the same.

'This mustn't be repeated. I'll never participate again—'

'I don't mix work with pleasure, or pleasure with emotional commitment. I don't *do* emotional commitment.' He spoke the words at the same time, and then looked at her sharply. 'What do you mean—?'

'Nothing.' She cut her hand through the air. Best to simply deal with this moment, and do so once and for all.

He *was* corporate. He *didn't* feel more than physical interest in her. She had somehow managed to embellish this encounter as if she believed his response to her ran deeper, and his words right now made that absolutely clear. *No commitment.*

She wanted to ask *Why not?* Instead, she forced out the words that had to be said.

'There was an attraction between us and we both gave in to it for a brief moment.' That should put it into perspective. 'It was a mistake and now it's over and done with. I'm sure we'll both very quickly forget it.'

'I'm sure you're right,' he agreed and left.

From: Kangagirl:
I was dumped very publicly by my fiancé in an office environment where we worked together. Now I'm up to my neck in one again. An office situation and lots of hard work, I mean, not anything else because I wouldn't be that silly. I feel pressured, that's all.

From: Englishcrumpet
What's your ex-fiancé's name and where can we find him in case we want to let him know what we think of him? The dirt bag!

From: Sanfrandani
Marissa. Do you still have feelings for the guy?

From: Kangagirl
No. I couldn't possibly have!

But Marissa hadn't been thinking of Michael Unsworth when she'd given her half desperate answer to her friends when they'd discussed last night's dinner. She'd been thinking of Rick. She placed several more loose letters and memos onto the pin inside the file on her desk and told herself not to think back to that kiss at all.

She needed to forget her boss in that way altogether and get back to her dating plans.

No distractions. Especially no Tall, Dark and Delicious distractions.

Tall, Out of Bounds and Emotionally Blockaded, she amended. All the things she could never accept. Except the tall part.

And *she* wasn't emotionally blockaded. She was cautious. A whole different matter.

Rick's mobile phone beeped out a message on his desk.

Marissa forced her attention to her work. What she really needed was for Tom to get better and come back so she could go back to working for Gordon, and stop thinking about Rick.

The fax machine whirred. Marissa got up at the same time that Rick left his desk. They met in front of the machine and hers was the hand that reached first for the sheet of paper that emerged.

'I'll take that. I think it'll be for me.' He reached out his hand.

'Certainly. Here you go.' She passed the fax to him, couldn't help but see the image of a head and shoulders that filled the space. A cheeky smile that belied the wounded expression in dark eyes. Arched brows and thick dark hair and a bit too much make-up on the face, if the black and white image was anything to go by. The girl looked about sixteen. His older niece?

Curiosity slid in sideways to assail her before she could stop it.

The office phone rang. With the fax clasped in his hand, Rick strode to her desk and answered it. 'Rick Morgan.' A pause. 'What's going on, Kirri?'

There was silence as he listened to whatever response he got and Marissa realised she was in the middle of the room, a party to a private conversation—something Rick wouldn't want her to overhear, if his reaction when she'd seen him with his other niece was any indication.

Marissa scooped a pile of files from the corner of her desk and headed for the file room. Rick's words followed her, as did that faxed image with the wounded eyes.

'You're as beautiful as ever, Kirri. You have

lovely blue eyes and a killer smile and you're sweet on the inside where it counts most of all. And so is your mother. You know that, Kirrilea.' His tone was both gentle and fierce. *Not* exactly emotionally blockaded right now!

He drew a breath and Marissa glanced out of the file room at him—just a really brief glimpse—but that one moment showed he was holding back some kind of deep inner anger, wanting to comfort his niece and not let her hear that anger in him, all at the same time. 'Next time don't ask Grandad something like that, okay? Ask me, instead.'

Another pause while Marissa started to push folders away and tried hard not to listen, not to wonder about this grandfather who wouldn't tell a teenager she looked lovely, about her boss's family altogether. Rick had said, 'Ask me.'

She bit her lip. He must have plenty of commitment capability, because he seemed to have it for his nieces, his sisters…

There were other things that week. A call from his mother. Final swimming lessons with his niece and the tinge of colour on the tips of his ears as he'd asked if Marissa might manage to make a certificate, perhaps with an image of a fish on it. Something to state that Julia had passed her first unofficial swimming class.

Marissa navigated each glimpse into his layers with the promise to herself that she wouldn't let them intrigue her. That she didn't want to help him unlock his inner ability to commit—she didn't even know if he truly possessed such a thing. *He* clearly believed he didn't. That she didn't think of his kiss constantly and wake in the middle of the night wondering what it would be like if they *did* live at the dawn of time, if she had chosen him.

Tick, tock, tick, tock.

No. No tick-tocking. No Big 3-0 depressive, subconscious birthday countdown, no biological rumblings at all, and no remembering kisses. No, no, no!

On Thursday, while Rick dictated straight over Marissa's shoulder to finalise a memo he didn't have time to even place first on a tape, a woman rushed through the door and zeroed her gaze onto him.

'I'm sorry. I'm probably interrupting, but something's happened and I don't have to take the chance because I know I committed to hostess duties for you tonight, Rick, and I'd never let you down, but I just wondered…'

The woman was thin, with a determined air about her, and she sported a feminine version of Rick's nose and jaw. She flipped straight brown hair over her shoulder and for a moment Marissa saw eyes very like the ones in that faxed photograph.

Marissa's interest—curiosity—spiked.

Anyone would be curious, she justified, and hated her weakness where her boss was concerned.

'What's happened, Darla?' Rick strode around the desk, clasped the woman's elbows. 'Is Kirrilea all right? Did our fath—'

'Kirri's fine, and Dad is his typical self. There's no point wishing he'll change because he's made it clear he won't, but I won't have him upsetting my daughter—' She broke off. 'I told Kirri to send you the fax. I hope you didn't mind.'

'I didn't.' He chopped a hand through the air as though to dismiss the very idea. 'Tell me what's brought you here.'

Marissa printed the memo Rick had dictated. 'If Rick can sign this I'll put the phone on answering service and hand-deliver the memo.

That way you won't be disturbed while I'm gone.' She would get out of their way and try not to think about his complexities. Or her ever-growing conviction that he had emotional commitment aplenty for his sisters and nieces and therefore why wouldn't he have the capacity for that in any other relationship?

'I'm so sorry. I'm Darla.' The woman stuck out her hand, shook Marissa's firmly. 'Forgive my rudeness. I was a little excited.'

Marissa liked Darla's honesty and her determined smile, the strength she sensed in her and, most of all, her clear affection for her brother.

'I'm Marissa. The borrowed secretary. Very transitory. And it's no problem.' Nor were the callisthenics of her brainwaves. Marissa would get those under control as of now. 'Please, excuse me.'

She took the signed memo, dealt with the phone, left them and delivered the memo.

Should she dawdle back to give them more time? It probably wasn't necessary. Rick would have taken his sister into his office.

He hadn't. They stood exactly where Marissa had left them. Darla was talking fast while Rick nodded.

Marissa's steps slowed as both heads turned her way. 'Um…'

Darla spoke first. 'Would you truly not mind the overtime, Marissa? Rick says you might be prepared to help him out, but I don't want to ask if it will cause any problems.'

Rick leaned a hand against the edge of Marissa's desk. Tension showed in the line of his shoulders and yet, when he looked at his sister, all Marissa could see was affection and…pride?

'My sister has the chance to meet with the central management team in charge of her real estate brokerage.' Rick's gaze met Marissa's and held. 'There may be a promotion in the offing…if you'd be prepared to hostess a business dinner at my home tonight.'

CHAPTER EIGHT

'OF COURSE. I'll be happy to hostess the event.' Marissa spoke the words while panic did its best to get a grip on her.

The business dinner at Rick's home had been noted in the BlackBerry. Everything went in there and, indeed, Marissa had prepared Rick some information so he could be fully informed before the evening. She'd thought that would be the extent of her involvement. The idea of spending a night working at Rick's side, in his home, in a whole other setting to the office, where she would see even more parts of him…well, it unnerved her even while her hormones set up a cheering section about it.

Marissa spoke to the other woman. 'If Rick feels I could be of assistance, I…I'm sure I can cope with hostessing the event.'

Somehow. Maybe. If she managed to get a grip on herself and her thoughts about her boss between now and then. Marissa tried to keep the hope out of her tone as she added, 'That is, if there's no one else more suitable, maybe someone else in the family who could take your place?'

'There isn't,' Rick said, squashing that hope quite flat.

A smile broke over Darla's face. 'Oh, thank you!'

The woman impulsively threw her arms around Marissa and then turned to her brother and hugged him. He cupped her head so tenderly in his hand as he hugged her back. A fierce well of protectiveness crossed his face before they separated.

Layers. How many more could he possibly have? Now Marissa's hormones had given up the cheer squad routine and brought out the tissues, going all emotional on her right when she didn't need that to happen.

'It's settled then.' Rick drew his wallet from his pocket and pulled out some notes, frowned when his sister opened her mouth. 'I know you like good luck charms. Buy one to wear tonight.' He gestured to the silver bracelet on her wrist. 'You'll find room for it on there somewhere. And get something for Kirrilea—a trinket. And tell her my secretary very kindly laminated that faxed page and I have it on my desk where I can enjoy it.'

Darla's fingers closed over the money and his hand, and a sheen of moisture came to her eyes before she blinked and turned away. 'God, I wish our father had half... Well...' She smiled with a fierce determination that quickly became the real thing as she turned once again to Marissa. 'Thank you. I hope I'll have good news after tonight but, even if not, I appreciate the chance to attend the meeting.'

She rushed out of the office at the same frenetic pace she'd entered it.

'If her speed is anything to go by, she probably does the work of five people and very much deserves a promotion.' Marissa made the observation lightly when she didn't feel light at all. But she would be okay tonight. *She would.*

'I know she deserves it.' He murmured the words without appearing to think about them.

There'd been no wedding band on Darla's finger, no mention of a man in the proceedings and an impression that Darla was alone and turned to her brother for emotional support.

Alone with a sixteen-year-old daughter. Darla hardly looked old enough. And Marissa now wanted to clutch at straws, even though some-thing told her that would be futile. 'Did you really need me to help you tonight, or did you just want Darla to feel free to chase this job promotion?'

Rick's eyelashes veiled his expression as he answered. 'There's no one else suitable at such short notice.'

'Right, then I guess that will be fine.' She would simply maintain her professionalism and make it fine. She could do that. All it would require was a little concentration, a lot of focus and maybe some tranquilliser for the hormone squad!

A phone call came in then. Marissa thought she recognised the voice, but couldn't place it. When she asked for a name, the caller paused for a heartbeat before saying, 'Just put me through. I'm returning his call.'

Marissa connected the call.

Rick rose from his desk and closed his door after he answered the call. Super-secret business, apparently.

Marissa got on with her work.

Whatever, anyway. She had more important things to think about. Like tonight!

* * *

'I think Carl Fritzer is deliberately goading you on the topic of environmental issues.' Marissa directed the comment to Rick and then nodded her thanks to the catering guru as she accepted a platter of artfully arranged biscotti and small handmade chocolates.

The evening was more over than started now, and the three of them stood in the kitchen of Rick's penthouse apartment. It was a large and lush place—four bedrooms at least and functional in all the nicest ways but, for tonight, Rick had taken everyone outside to the rooftop terrace.

Marissa had fought with herself every step since she'd arrived. She didn't want to be delighted by his home, nor constantly and utterly aware of him in it. Didn't want to note that his midnight-blue shirt and black trousers made him look even more Tall, Mysterious and Compelling. She still wanted Ordinary, darn it. She did!

'I truly don't understand why Mr Fritzer would do that.' *Focus on work, Marissa.* 'What difference does it make to any possible business dealings between our company and his?' The stamp of ownership she put on her statement was a whole new problem. Since when had it been the 'Marissa and Rick team'?

Remember what happened to the 'Michael and Marissa' so-called 'team'? Well, you should!

Marissa forced herself to go on. 'Morgan's follows all the codes to the letter and, in a lot of cases, goes a lot further than most companies in its efforts towards environmental friendliness.'

'The man seems to consider a bit of goading as good entertainment value, but I noticed his colleagues don't seem to share his enthusiasm for the topic.' When Rick shrugged, his shirt clung to his broad shoulders, outlined the strength of the muscles beneath the cloth.

There was something different in him tonight when he looked at her, too. She couldn't pin it down, but he seemed to be weighing her up, or searching for something. He was perhaps softer towards her? More attentive? Interested in a different way?

Some of his examination seemed—she didn't know—almost empathetic or something? But that made no sense.

What if he *was* beginning to think of her in a deeper way? Given her determination to steer utterly clear of even noticing him, the thought shouldn't please her, yet she felt a reciprocal softening towards him.

'There may be something Fritzer is hiding about his own dealings or standards.' Rick's gaze caressed her face and neck as he went on. Did he realise he was doing that? 'I'll have a team investigate that possibility before I commit us to any work with the company. I can find out anything I need to know before they get to the stage of an acceptance of our offer of services.'

He hesitated and a combination of unease and knowledge, awareness and that same empathy flared in his eyes again. For a moment Marissa thought he would reach for her, right there in front of the caterer…

'Is that coffee? Just what's needed.' One of the female business delegates strolled inside. 'Can I help with anything?'

'I think we have it under control.' A frown crossed Rick's face before he lifted the tray of coffees.

Disappointment surged through Marissa and she told herself not to be foolish, forced her attention to the drinks Rick held on the tray.

The lattes bore everything from starfish shapes to mini Harbour Bridges in the foam tops. He thanked the caterer. 'The rest we can manage for ourselves, if you're happy to let yourself out?'

The young man scooped up a backpack from the corner of the kitchen. 'Cheers. It was a pleasure to help you, as always.' He strode to the apartment's front door and left.

They returned to the West Australian business delegation of men and women where they sat in big squashy outdoor chairs grouped around low tables.

Rick's apartment and exclusive terrace took up the entire top level of the building. The formal outdoor dining area seated up to twenty people. They'd eaten there with city views all around them and the lush foliage of the rooftop garden behind them. The sight and scent of flowers and plants and shrubs filled the area. Roses and mint, hardy native shrubs mixed with hydrangeas and mat-rush and Easter cactus.

His home was truly gorgeous and Marissa couldn't help but appreciate the beauty. He wore his wealth very comfortably here. He'd seemed pleased when she'd first arrived and admired his apartment and surroundings.

It was also a large enough home, and secure enough, that a small family could thrive quite nicely here if necessary. A house with a full garden would be better, of course, but children could enjoy the terrace garden, or be taken to play in the large park right across the road from the building...

Oh, what was she thinking? She had to focus on the business of the evening, not fantasies that were becoming more and more difficult to quash.

'Well, it's a lovely evening for a business function and this is the perfect setting for it.' She caught Rick's eye and gestured with her hand, but all that did was draw their attention to the fact that darkness had now fallen and, beyond the well-lit terrace, the city lights, Lavender Bay, the Harbour Bridge, and buildings of all shapes and sizes glittered before them.

The setting was romantic. Her hormones had recognised this immediately, even if Marissa had been busy trying not to notice the fact.

Why couldn't she stop viewing her employer in this way? Stop herself from developing a deeper and deeper interest in him when she knew that doing so was utterly futile? Was it because she felt she knew Rick better now? Somehow, she'd started to trust him as she'd watched him care for his sisters and nieces and saw his business dealings, which were far more frank than Michael Unsworth's behaviour had been in the workplace, or out of it.

'Well, here's the coffee, everyone,' she called. 'Actually, it's coffee *art*, with thanks to our now departed caterer.' She pushed the memories of Michael away and tried not to think about her shifting feelings towards her boss. Rick was much more difficult to dismiss than thoughts of Michael, and that knowledge was not comforting.

Rick didn't want any kind of emotional commitment. He hadn't said why, but he'd made that fact clear. She suspected it had to do with his father, or his family life generally, but what did it matter in the end? Her boss didn't want *her*. Maybe she should simply be grateful he was being honest about that. She started to hand out the drinks.

Rick watched Marissa hostess the small group, chatting as she went, and he thought about her use of the term 'we,' as though she felt as invested in the company as he did. He couldn't forget kissing her, nor reconcile himself to the shift inside him that had somehow been different from anything he had experienced before.

She looked beautiful tonight, all soft curves beneath the golden dress, her hair up and her nape tantalisingly bare. He wanted to press his lips to that soft skin, to somehow pay homage to her.

Thoughts battered at him. She looked right here—in his home. He wanted to keep her here. And other thoughts—of taking her to his bedroom, closing the door on the world and staying there with her until he knew all of her, understood all of her and she'd given all of herself to him. How could he want that when he would never give her the same in return?

Maybe he didn't want it. Not really. Couldn't this all be about lust and the confusion of feeling this way towards a woman he was working with and coming to admire in a working environment?

The business talk moved on. Fritzer goaded a little more, and Rick ignored it. He sat at Marissa's side, his arm stretched across the back of her chair in a gesture he knew was possessive, but he couldn't make himself stop it. He needed to be near her, close enough to touch even if he didn't.

Yes. He was in trouble, but he could control it. He must be able to do at least that.

Over coffee, talk turned to what the city had to offer.

One of the women leaned forward. 'We have half of tomorrow before we leave. I'm wondering what to do with the time.'

'There's plenty on offer in terms of entertainment, shopping, whatever you like, really.' Rick stretched out his legs, stared at the neat crease in the dark trousers. Imagined the gold of Marissa's dress against the fabric.

All roads led back to it. The fact that he wanted Marissa—still wanted her.

'You might consider the new animal petting zoo.' Marissa spoke the words to the other woman. Her gaze met Rick's and a delicate flush rose in her cheeks as she seemed to wish she hadn't raised the topic.

She went on, waved her hand. 'Holding a koala is a unique experience.'

And then he remembered *that* moment, the trembling of her shoulders and the rush of protective instinct that had coursed through him, had tapped into instincts he'd been ignoring ever since that moment.

'The koalas smell of eucalyptus oil, don't they, Marissa?' *Keep it light. That's all it can be.* 'Did you manage to wash the scent out of that cardigan?'

'I did get the cardigan clean, and I imagine our overseas visitors probably made good use of a dry-cleaner's after that visit.' Marissa lowered her gaze to her coffee cup. 'We've had some interesting moments during my brief time filling in as your assistant.'

Maybe she wanted to remind them both that this wouldn't last. That soon she would go back to her regular job and he wouldn't see more of her than a glimpse in a corridor from time to time. Maybe he should be glad she wanted to remind him of that.

Instead, a kaleidoscope of images and moments spent with her bombarded his mind and his senses. Marissa with a hard hat squashed over her curly hair that day on the bridge. Presenting him with a laminated certificate for his niece for completing her swimming lessons. Cursing at the photocopier beneath her breath when she thought he couldn't hear her.

He wanted Tom back on his feet but the thought of Marissa easing back to the periphery of his working life didn't sit well with him.

'We should go.'

'Yes, it's been a productive evening.'

'We'll take a vote with the full group and you'll hear from us.'

One by one their guests stood. It took another few minutes for Rick to see them completely out and away.

When Rick closed the door finally on the guests, Marissa moved to the terrace to collect the empty cups and return them to the kitchen. She turned as he joined her.

'I'll get the biscotti tray.' And then she needed to leave, to forget this glimpse into yet another side to her boss.

'Leave it for now.' He poured two glasses of liqueur, passed one to her and led her to the edge of the terrace with his hand on her arm.

'I guess we deserve five minutes to celebrate this evening's hard work. To enjoy the view now it's quiet and there's time to focus on it.' She couldn't help the observation that followed. 'Somehow I'd expected your apartment to be all chrome and black and sharp lines with the view carefully shut outside through long planes of plate glass. The terrace entertainment area surprised me. It's lovely.'

'I'm pleased you like it.' His gaze darkened on her, again seemed to search inside her.

Would he be as pleased to know she'd imagined it being a home to a family? No. He wouldn't, would he? She lifted the glass and inhaled the aroma of the drink. 'I smell spices and tea and rum. And vanilla?'

'It's Voyant Chai Cream. I think you'll like it.' He watched her over the rim of his glass as they sipped.

'Very smooth.' She sipped again. Savoured. Tried hard not to think about the war going on inside her body that shouldn't be going on at all, and especially not where Rick was concerned.

For the first time in her life Marissa was subjected to forces of her own nature, her own hidden needs, which she had never even considered she might struggle to control. She couldn't seem to stop herself from associating some of those desires with her boss. She forced her attention back to the drink in her hand. 'It's delicious.'

'Yes.' The single word seemed to wrap around her, be meant for her. All he did was match her sip for sip before he finally set his glass down, tucked his hands in his pockets and looked out over the harbour, and yet she felt his desire for her as though he'd spoken it aloud.

'It was a good night, don't you think?' He glanced at her, the heat in his eyes partially concealed, but very much there. Talked business as they should be doing. 'Despite that bit of goading, I expect they'll sign with us for their project.'

'It was—yes. I believe it was a successful evening.' She set her glass down with trembling fingers.

The softness of the city night cast his face in clarity and shadows. Just like the man. She had to pull herself together, to play this out the safe way, to keep her focus on their working relationship and not these odd, nebulous things she wanted that she didn't even know if she could ever have.

She should put herself to sleep or something until she'd passed her birthday, get it behind her so she could realise it hadn't changed anything, that she was the same inside and she didn't have to pine for a family of her own.

'In part, that success is thanks to you.' He let his gaze roam over her face. 'I think you captured all of them.' His hands fell to his sides. She thought he murmured, 'You captivated me.'

A long beat of silence followed as she fought with herself. Finally she spoke. 'I should go. Tomorrow is another working day.' Maybe if she reminded herself of that she wouldn't respond to him quite so much.

Marissa moved away from the view, from the sparkle of city lights. They stepped inside and she collected her bag from the kitchen. 'I'll get the doorman to organise me a cab straight off the rank downstairs.'

'I'll take you down.'

'There's no need.' She drew a breath as they paused before his door. 'Goodnight, Rick. I'm glad I could help. I hope your sister gets the job promotion. I got the impression it would mean a lot if she did.'

'Darla deserves the break. She's worked hard for that company for many years, first as a part-timer and working up to full-time once Kirrilea started school.'

'You're proud of her. Of your niece, too.' She faced him before the closed door, searched his eyes.

'They're easy people to be proud of.' Rick reached past her to open the door. His fingers wrapped around the doorknob.

And the tension wrapped right around them, too.

'Back away from me, Marissa. Tell me not to mess with a perfectly good working relationship. Tell me not to mess with you.'

'You've been different tonight.' She whispered the words and he braced his feet and drew her into the V of his body.

Her hand lifted to his chest and he kissed her. Pressed his mouth to hers and his body to hers, and pleasure and a feeling rightness swept through her.

'More.' He whispered the word.

Marissa lost herself so thoroughly in Rick's kiss, lost senses and feelings and responses and, yes, emotions, in him. When his lips left hers to trail over her ear to the sensitive cord of her neck, she closed her eyes and let the feel of his body against hers, his hands cupping her head, her shoulders so sweetly, sweep through her.

Could a man's touch communicate straight to the heart of not only a woman's senses, but also her soul? It seemed so.

She clasped her hands on his shoulders, curled her fingers around his upper arms and held on. When he skirted his hands up from her waist, over her back, to where her shoulders were bared by the wide cowl neck of the dress, she shivered.

A strained, needy sound passed through his lips. It was the last thing she consciously registered for long moments as they stood by his door, their bodies tightly entwined, her resistance and grand plans in shambles. Her bag lay at her feet. She had no idea when it had landed there.

'Say my name.' The words were harsh and possessive, demanding and enervating. 'I want to hear it. I don't want you to be thinking of him—'

What did he mean? A chill rushed over her skin and all through her body. She wrenched away from him. 'What do you know? What have you heard? About that fake engagement I believed was real? About Michael—'

'Ah, I didn't mean to say that.' He pushed a hand through his hair. 'I had to know why you left your last job, Marissa.' His eyes were dark and turbulent. 'The information about your personal life—I didn't ask for it, I stopped the man when I realised where he was headed with the conversation but by then it was too late.'

'Right. I see. So you phoned my old company to investigate why I left, and you found out things about me at that time.' If his gaze softened into pity she would die right there, and now it all made sense. This. This was the empathy he'd displayed earlier.

'Without meaning to find those things out, yes.' He seemed to search for words.

Apology. Regret.

Yes, she heard them in his tone but, most of all, she heard that he knew of that embarrassment. He now probably thought she was desperate and on a manhunt. What if he thought she'd set out to hunt *him*? Mortification, shame and anger crashed through her. She clutched at the anger because the others were too awful to bear.

'That call. I knew I recognised the voice.' And Rick had closed his office door and talked about her. 'I don't care if you say it was business.' Her voice shook. 'I'd started to trust you. I can't believe I did. What did the man tell you? That Michael Unsworth made a fool of me? What does that have to do with my good record at Morgan's?'

'Nothing. I didn't want that information. I didn't ask for it.' He reached for her hand but she drew back.

He went on in a low voice, 'I'm sorry he hurt you, Marissa.'

'Well, don't be sorry because I am totally over

the way Michael treated me. I learned from it and I moved on. Was that what this kiss was about? Pity? Tell me!'

He drew a harsh breath into his lungs. 'You know better than that. I want you in my bed and I have from the first day I had you up on that excuse for a bridge with me. Maybe you should pity *me*, because I can't seem to get that desire for you out of my system, no matter what I do.'

Rick's admission stunned Marissa into silence. More, perhaps, because of the flash of something deeper than desire that burned for a moment in his gaze before he masked it.

Oh, will you listen to yourself, Marissa? Do you want to fall for Mr Corporate a second time?

Rick had just *proved* his ruthlessness to her!

But he'd also apologised and seemed as though he meant it.

She scooped her bag from the floor. 'I just want us to work together and get along and I want to follow my well thought out plans for my life in peace. Is that so much to want?'

'It isn't. It isn't too much to want.' He took a step towards her as she wrenched open the door. 'Marissa—'

But she didn't wait to hear what he might have said.

She left.

CHAPTER NINE

To: Sanfrandani, Englishcrumpet
From: Kangagirl
One last thing to tell you both. I spoke to Mum on the phone early this morning. We had a good talk and I let her know I'd rather spend a weekend with her and Dad a bit down the track after my birthday, that I'm really busy at the moment and don't want a party of any kind.

From: Englishcrumpet
I'm sure your mum will understand.

From: Sanfrandani
You can throw a big party when you're ready.

From: Englishcrumpet
Or not.

From: Kangagirl
People make a big deal out of the thirtieth birthday, but really, it's just another day on the calendar. I probably won't even think much about it at all.

Grace had instant messaged a little after that, a message Marissa caught on her way out the door to go to work. She'd asked whether Marissa was in denial about her thirtieth birthday.

Marissa hadn't had time to respond. And right now she was focused on other things. Rick Morgan things, to be precise. Work things. Marissa barrelled along the corridor towards Rick's suite of offices.

Anyway, she had to come to terms with that looming birthday. It wasn't denial to say it wasn't significant, it was the power of positive statement. Say it enough times and she'd come to believe it.

If she could apply the same outlook to her relationship with Rick—her *working only* relationship—that would be a great help.

As a mature professional, she could work with Rick until his secretary returned. She only had to survive that long and then she could forget him, forget what he knew about her. All she needed to do was hold her head up and he'd soon realise he had no reason to pity her.

Dani and Grace had blamed last night's kiss on too much alcohol or maybe an overload of successful business-related feeling when Marissa had calmly and casually discussed the topic with them via two separate Instant Message sessions last night and this morning—before she'd sent that later message about Mum and avoiding a birthday party.

You mean when you buzzed them, desperate for some support because you were scared stiff you'd let yourself fall for the boss only to find out he'd invaded your privacy?

She had *not* fallen for the boss, nor did she intend to. And he *had* invaded her privacy.

He's head of a multi-million dollar company and you've been working directly for him, handling some very sensitive material. He exercised his right to enquire about your past employment and he said he only *wanted to know about that. You know the department head who spoke to him is a big gossip.*

Marissa had worked out the identity of the caller, of course. It had only taken the jolt of discovering that Rick had gone after the information for her to remember the owner of that somehow familiar voice.

Okay, fine, there was that. But she still didn't have to like it or feel comfortable. Rick *did* know her secret.

Perhaps he hadn't acted inappropriately, and he had seemed to truly regret the outcome. And she knew one of his secrets. That he wanted to make love to her, had desired her from Day One.

That knowledge did not thrill or tempt her. She couldn't let it!

Her initial IM sessions with Dani and Grace hadn't been the result of a desperate buzzing, either. More of a, *Hello, if you're there a talk might be nice but no problem if you're not* kind of buzzing. An, *I don't need help or anything. Just felt like chatting* sort of buzzing.

They were all friends. Grace had already confessed that she was concerned about her daughter Daisy going off on her gap year backpacking around Europe and Dani had admitted she had financial pressures and was worried about paying off her student loans from college and graduate school.

Marissa had owed it to them to contribute her share to the confidence stakes, and so she had admitted that she might be having a teensy tiny issue with awareness of her boss. Nothing dramatic. Certainly nothing to worry about. She could put it to rights.

Grace had been the voice of reason, had encouraged Marissa not to blame Rick too much for his accidental knowledge of her past. Dani had been a little silent on the subject, but certainly sympathetic. They'd swapped mailing addresses and phone numbers after their chats, and Marissa had visited the early opening post shop this morning and sent them both some gifts.

Chocolate. Australian chocolate, to be exact, because chocolate lifted your spirits and gave you confidence.

Because her friends might enjoy it, and Marissa did not need courage to face Rick again, even if she had eaten a chocolate bar this morning while mailing the others. All in all, she was dealing very well with her life right now.

She hadn't even thought about that knitting idea for the past couple of days. Not really. Other than to look at the wool, wondering about the exact blend of lemon and pink and blue of the variegated strands…

Marissa shoved open the door to the office suite.

'Good morning, Rick.' She spoke his name in a firm, even, totally in control and not at all kissed senseless or embarrassed or overwrought tone as she crossed the office space at a fast clip.

Stride in. Purposefully get to work. Keep it impersonal and he would soon see she was not at all carrying any scars from the past.

No? So why did you let that past dictate the kind of man you want in your future?

Because she'd learned from her mistake!

'Thank you, Collins. I appreciate you bringing that to my attention.' Rick's voice was pitched in a businesslike tone that had absolutely nothing to do with Marissa's greeting or, indeed, with her at all.

Because he wasn't alone, was he? How unprofessional of her to just storm in and start yammering away without even looking. Well, she'd only said good morning, but even so…

Concentrate, Marissa. If professionalism at all times is going to be your motto, you might start with attention to detail. Such as—who might be with your boss when you enter the office.

She hurried to her desk as Rick and the other man headed out of Rick's room. Right. Marissa set about sorting her in-tray's contents into 'Get it done early', 'Can wait until later this morning' and 'Yeah, sure she'd really get to this today. Not!' piles on her desk. The laminate covered in cartoons quickly disappeared beneath the piles of work. She wasn't in the mood to be amused anyway.

Rick saw his visitor out. The man gave Marissa a nod in passing. And then Rick turned to her and yanked at his tie and a wealth of regret showed in his eyes as he seemed to search for words.

'About last night...' He cleared his throat. 'About my investigating why you'd left your last position, I mean...'

'I overreacted.'

Please accept that as the truth, and please don't bring up the kiss that led to that discussion.

'My reaction was silly because that piece of past history is exactly that. I've moved on. I'm dating, at least casually, again—looking for a nice, ordinary guy. Let's just forget all of it. That's what I'd like the most at this point.'

If her request rang hollow, she hoped he didn't note it. And if his gaze remained as dark and uncertain as before, she couldn't let herself think about that. Professionalism at all times. She couldn't let there be anything else.

Rick's gaze searched hers before he nodded and murmured, 'I'm pleased you're prepared to forget it.' He didn't *look* pleased, but really, what would she know?

The next couple of hours passed in a flurry of the usual busyness. Rick worked on, but he had a hard time concentrating. He wanted to go out to Marissa, tell her again that he was truly sorry, somehow make up for the way he'd invaded her privacy. He didn't want to think of her 'dating casually' and how possessive and inappropriate was that?

'I was wondering, after everything, if Darla got the promotion? I meant to ask earlier but I...got distracted.' Marissa asked the question from his office doorway, and he looked up into brown eyes that had melted for him last night, had filled with warmth and delightful response before he'd ruined it all with his thoughtless words.

Ruined what couldn't be allowed to happen

anyway. Maybe he should just be grateful that something had put a stop to where that kiss had been headed. And forget about her 'dating' plans. 'Darla got the promotion. I'm taking her and Kirri out during Kirri's school lunch break today to celebrate.'

'I'm really happy for her. Please pass on my congratulations to your sister when you see her.' Marissa turned away and went back to her desk and her work.

That was as it should be, right?

So why did Rick feel so empty inside, as though he'd almost grasped something special in his hands, only to have it slip away after all?

What was the matter with him? He pushed himself back into his work and tried not to think beyond it.

Marissa observed her boss's concentration on his work and tried her best to emulate it. She didn't want to think. About his complex family. About him at all.

The hours came and went and, late in the afternoon, after a quiet lull of concentrating solely on her work uninterrupted, the phone rang. She took the call, put it through to Rick. 'You have a call on line one. It's Tom.'

Rick murmured his thanks and she went on with her work.

'Tom.' His voice softened. 'How are you?'

Another phone line rang. As she reached for it, Rick said, 'Just rest and do whatever the doctor tells you, Tom. If it's another two weeks, so be it. Marissa—Marissa's holding the fort well enough in your absence.'

Marissa tuned out Rick's voice and answered the second call. 'Marissa Warren.'

'Marissa, it's Dad.' His voice was strained as he went on. 'Mum's in the hospital, love, with quite bad abdominal pain. They're doing tests right now and they're going to send her for an ultrasound before they—' He cleared his throat. 'To see what's wrong.'

'I'll come straight away, Dad. Is Aunty Jean—?' Panic flooded through her and she couldn't remember what she'd been going to ask.

'Yes, Jean's on her way.' Her father drew a breath. 'She should be here in another hour.'

'Good. That's good.' Marissa had to get to Milberry. It was her only thought as she clutched the phone tighter in her hand. 'You can't use your cellphone inside the hospital, I know, but you'll phone my cell once Mum's back from the tests, let me know if there's anything—?'

Marissa was in trouble. Rick ended his call with Tom and reached her desk before he realised he'd moved. As she raised her eyes and locked onto his, something deep inside him clenched.

'If there needs to be an operation they might move her to a larger hospital in another town.' Marissa paused and listened again. 'Yes, I understand we don't know enough at this stage. I'll just set off, Dad. You're right. That's all I can do for now. I love you. When you see Mum again, tell her I love her and I'm on my way.'

The moment she replaced the phone, Rick spoke.

'What do you need?' Whatever it was, he would get it for her, do it for her. The decision was instinctive. He didn't want to examine the significance of it, could only worry for the woman in front of him. 'Where's your mother? Let me know the fastest way you can be at her side and I'll make it happen.'

Marissa was already on her feet, her hand in the drawer to retrieve her bag when she stopped, looked up at him. She blinked hard and her mouth worked. 'Mum was rushed to hospital in all this pain.'

'What happened to her, sweetheart?' The endearment slipped out, perhaps as unnoticed by its recipient as it was unplanned by him.

Her brown eyes darkened. 'I only know it was abdominal pain. The ambulance had to get her from the newsagent's while Dad came back in from his work on one of the roadworks crews outside of town. Dad only got to see her for a second before they took her away, and they wouldn't tell him much. I have to get to Milberry. I need the Mini.'

'The car you hire from your neighbour.' He remembered her muttering something about that, the day she'd felt faint after their crisis meeting.

It felt so long ago, and a Mini wasn't the vehicle to get her out of the city and to her family with any kind of speed or comfort.

Rick caught her wrist between his fingers, rubbed his thumb across the soft skin. Hoped the touch offered some comfort, and silently acknowledged that a part of him wanted the right to more, whether that meant his emotions were involved in her, or not.

He couldn't worry about any of that now. 'Do

any flights go to the township? I only know of it vaguely. It's rather off the beaten path, isn't it? How far is it by road? I can charter a plane for you if there's an airstrip...'

'There are no flights, no airstrip. Milberry doesn't have an airport. It's a reasonable sized town but there's nothing much around it.' Marissa stared at the mess on her desk as though she didn't know what to do with it, and then she stared at him as though she wasn't quite sure what to do with his offer either. 'It'll take me almost three hours in the Mini. Mum's been at the hospital about an hour already, I think.'

'I'll take you myself—'

'I forgot. My neighbour left Sydney this morning with the Mini.' She broke off and said in confusion, 'You'll take me?'

'My car will be faster than a Mini, faster than you having to hire something.' He wanted to beg her to let him do this for her. Instead, he made it a statement and silently urged her to simply agree with it. 'We can leave straight away.'

Confusion clouded her worried brown eyes. 'You can't... I can't ask...'

'I can, and I'm not asking you to ask.' *He* needed permission. Needed to be allowed, wanted to draw her into his arms and promise her everything would be all right, that he would fix everything for her. 'Give me one minute and we're out of here.'

He used that minute to get on the phone and instruct one of the senior staff to come in and pack the office up for them and secure everything.

His borrowed secretary was in trouble. He could help her and he'd chosen to do so. That didn't have to be any big thing, and his relief as Marissa put herself in his hands and allowed him to usher her from the building was simply that of a man who had got his way.

He told himself all this, but the intensity he felt inside didn't lessen.

In moments he had Marissa out of the office building, into his ground-eating vehicle and away. A glance showed that her face hadn't regained any colour. She was also utterly silent. 'Tell me the route.'

She gave him the directions and fell silent again.

Rick clenched his hands around the wheel and got them clear of the city. Once he had, he murmured her name and reached for her hand. He curled his fingers around hers and she cast a glance his way.

'Move into the middle seat so we can talk while I drive.' He tugged on her hand. 'You're going to tell me everything your father said, the name of the hospital your mother is in and all you know about her situation.'

She obeyed him without question, and that told him, more clearly than anything else, the extent of her concern for her mother.

Once he had her shoulder pressed against his arm, her body close enough to feel her warmth and know she could feel his warmth, Rick relaxed marginally.

'Talk, Marissa.' He stroked his fingers over hers, registered the tremble that spoke of her tension.

'Dad said they were sending her for an ultrasound of the abdominal area.' She drew a deep breath. 'There's a small imaging facility in Milberry that does that sort of thing and they were opening it up for her. I guess the place must close at five. That would have meant another ambulance trip, though a short one.

'Dad wanted to go with them but the nursing staff said no. I suppose they needed to focus on finding out what…what needed to be done after the tests.' Her breath hitched as she ended this speech.

Rick squeezed her hand, drew it onto his thigh and curled his fingers over hers. 'There are lots of things that can cause pain that are not life-threatening. If it was her appendix, for example, an operation should set it to rights.'

She nodded. 'Maybe that's what it is.'

'How old is your mother? Has she enjoyed good health until now?'

'She's fifty. She never gets sick. Not like this. Neither of them do.' Suddenly the fingers beneath his curled with tension. 'What if…'

'What if we ring the hospital and ask if there's any news?' He inserted the question gently.

Marissa tugged her bag from the floor by its strap. Her fingers were curled beneath Rick's, against his strong thigh. She couldn't seem to make herself let go or shift away. She didn't want to leave the comfort of that press of warmth against her shoulder and arm.

Rick *wasn't* Michael Unsworth. He wasn't anything like her ex-fiancé. That knowledge was probably even more cause for worry, but right now she only had room to worry about Mum.

She lifted her phone. A moment later she had the hospital on the line.

'It's Marissa Warren. My mother…' she

cleared her throat '…my mother, Matilda Warren, arrived by ambulance with abdominal pain. I'd like to know how she is.'

'Your mother is still under examination,' the woman on the end of the line said briskly. 'She's had several tests done and Doctor is with her now. We'll know more in a little while. Are you on your way to see her, dear? There might be more news if you leave it another half hour or so…'

'We're only about another hour away now.' Rick murmured the words.

She glanced at him, realised she'd ended the call and simply sat there with the phone in her hand.

'I've taken it for granted that they're there, in good health…' She trailed off.

'Then keep believing in that good health. And if she needs anything that I can arrange or help with, to be airlifted to a different hospital in a private helicopter or anything…'

'I hope she won't need that, but I appreciate your words.' She swallowed hard and her fingers flexed beneath his as she registered just how much his concern meant to her.

She couldn't think about that now, couldn't

see his actions as a sign of his ability to care, or commit. 'We'll lose phone reception for a while about half an hour out of Milberry. I may not get to hear the test results until we're close to town.' Her gaze tracked over him despite herself. 'There's an area that doesn't pick up very well.'

'You should make any other calls now before we lose reception.'

'Yes, I'd better do that.' How did Rick feel about holding her hand? Had he simply wanted to offer comfort? It felt somehow deeper than that, and he was so determined to help her, anything she might need...

He glanced her way. 'Did you want to try your father again?'

'No. Dad won't have his phone on inside the hospital, but I'd like to send a message to one of my friends.' She toyed with her phone. 'Yes, I think Grace would be out of bed by now, or at least close to it.'

She'd also arranged a drink after work with a man from the dating site. Marissa looked up his number in her phone listings—just as well she'd put it in there—and sent a quick message explaining her situation. Doing that made her aware, finally, of how close she was pressed to

Rick's side, how much she'd been leaning on him, physically and emotionally.

'I'm sorry. I'm not usually so…needy.' She moved away to the passenger seat.

'You weren't.' He cast a glance at her that revealed warmth and caring in the depths of his eyes. 'There's nothing wrong with leaning on someone else sometimes.'

Marissa's phone gave a number of beeps and she quickly glanced at it. 'Two messages.'

She checked the first message. 'This one's from my friend Grace in London, well, an Internet friend, actually. She says, "Be strong, sweetie, and hugs and prayers for your mum. Grace xx." Grace has a nineteen-year-old daughter and has lived a complete different life to me in so many ways, yet I feel a connection with her. Knowing her is kind of like having a fun older sister.'

'What about the other message?'

She didn't really want to tell him about the man she'd planned to meet for a drink. Why had she bothered anyway? The thought rolled over her, and she did her best to push it away. Right now wasn't the time to try to figure out whether she was wasting her time on the dating site, whether her reasons for joining were even right…

Marissa opened the message reluctantly, and then relaxed. 'This is from another of my Internet friends, Dani. Grace must have forwarded my message to her. I didn't want to wake Dani.' She read the second message out. '"Sending prayers. Call me if you need 2. Any time!!!"'

'Where does Dani live? Is she an older woman like Grace?'

'San Francisco, and no. She's younger than I am and more ambitious in certain ways. Well, perhaps not *more ambitious*, but highly focused in her working life particularly, I think. Dani is at the start of her career and she's studied hard and really wants to have a great job. At the moment she's working in some dead end position she doesn't like to talk about and hoping something better will come along.'

'Do you have sisters or brothers, Marissa?'

He'd probably asked to keep her mind occupied. Marissa wanted to open up to him anyway. As she recognised that, she stared out of the window at the scenery flashing by.

Grassy paddocks on either side of the road interspersed with native gum and paper-bark trees. Hills undulated as far as the eye could see and gave a sense of quiet and open space very different from the teeming life of the city.

They weren't too far from Milberry now. What would he think of her home town?

'No sisters or brothers. I'm an only child. Maybe that's why I want...' She broke off, cleared her throat. 'Mum and Dad only ever had me, but Mum made sure I had lots of chances to play with other children, to get the social interaction I needed. What about you? Just the two sisters?'

'Yes. I'm the eldest. Darla's in the middle, and Faith is the youngest.'

And his sisters had married, made families, but Rick hadn't.

Minutes passed. Marissa clutched her phone and willed it to ring.

'There's the ten kilometre sign.' She stiffened in her seat and, as though their nearness had brought it about, her phone finally complied with a ring tone. With a gasp, she fumbled for it and quickly answered.

'Yes. Yes. Okay. All right. I can't wait to see her.'

While Marissa paused to listen to her caller, Rick slowed at the outskirts of the township.

'We'll see you soon, Dad.' She ended the call and sat forward to give Rick directions.

CHAPTER TEN

'WE'RE to go straight to Mum and Dad's unit. I don't know what to think!' Marissa's words tumbled out in a rush, concern warring with threads of relief she couldn't truly believe. Not yet. 'They've let Mum go home with my Aunty Jean to watch over her. Aunty's a registered nurse.'

'How could they release her so quickly after such pain?' Rick put the question that was filling her thoughts into words. 'What was the diagnosis? Is this a decent hospital we're talking about? If not, we'll get her admitted somewhere else.'

'Apparently a cyst ruptured on one of Mum's ovaries. She is still in some discomfort but it's not severe now. They say she just needs to rest with the appropriate medication. Once they were certain of the diagnosis they let her go.'

Marissa drew a quick breath. 'It is a good hospital, the staff are reliable and Aunty Jean wouldn't let them release her unless she was confident Mum was up to that. Even so, I need to see her. If I look at her, I'll know—'

'How do we get to your parents' home?' He gestured ahead of them. 'Let's get you there so you can see for yourself.'

'If you follow this road it will take you straight through the main street of the town.' He understood what she needed and that…warmed her. 'After the Region's Own Bank building you turn left and Mum and Dad's unit is in the second street on the right.'

His gaze glanced left and right as he followed the directions she'd given him.

Many of the homes were red brick or weatherboard with corrugated iron roofs. Just about every front garden had rose bushes or camellias, a front fence with a wrought iron gate with an old-fashioned curlicue scroll design on top, and a mailbox on the right-hand gatepost.

There were vintage cars interspersed with sedans and utility trucks in the main street.

A rally weekend, Marissa realised vaguely, and sat forward in her seat again as they neared the turn to her parents' home.

'That's their place.' She pointed. 'The small

pale brick one with the red sedan and green station wagon parked out front.'

Rick followed Marissa's directions and parked on the street behind the other two cars. He studied the workmanship of the square building design, with its regulation small porch, front window awnings and slightly curved pathway from the front fence to that porch, but his thoughts were focused on the woman at his side.

He'd expected Marissa to leap from the vehicle before he'd even parked it properly. Instead, at the last minute, she turned to face him.

Her eyes were wide, her expression a combination of concern and chagrin. 'I haven't thanked you for dropping everything to get me here the way you did and for your kindness during the trip. It…well… I hope Mum truly is a lot better, though I'm still concerned for her, and I appreciate—'

'I know you do, and there's no need to say anything.' Maybe she was hesitating at the last moment out of fear of what she would find. If so, the sooner she saw her Mum the better. He opened his door and came to her side to help her out.

With her hand clasped in his as he helped her

down, he admitted, 'I wanted to bring you.' He'd needed to, in the same way he'd needed to fix things for Darla over the years, for Faith.

No. Not the same. This was different.

Yes. It's more than those urges have ever been.

He didn't want to think that. Their gazes met and held for a brief moment and something flared between them. She did fly up the path then, and rapped on the door even as it opened from inside.

Rick followed more slowly and watched as a man with thinning grey-streaked dark hair pulled Marissa into his arms and held her tight. The comfort given and exchanged in their hug caught at something inside Rick and his chest hurt as he acknowledged the deep closeness playing out in front of him.

'Dad, this is the boss of Morgan's, Rick Morgan. I told you and Mum I'm working for him while his secretary is on sick leave and Gordon is on holiday.' Marissa rushed the words out and then her voice softened. 'Rick, please meet my father, Abraham Warren, but he prefers Abe.'

Did Marissa's face soften on *his* name? It had seemed to and while something inside Rick took the thought in a stranglehold and refused to let it go, heat rode the back of his neck as he shook the older man's hand and murmured a greeting.

He was concerned. He needed Marissa to see her mother and feel assured that the woman would be okay. It wasn't anything else. Certainly not some misguided and misplaced hope that Marissa's father would approve—*like*—him.

'Thank you for bringing Marissa to us.' Abe stepped back. If he noticed anything odd in Rick's demeanour, he didn't show it.

Rick wished he had some of the same self-control.

Abe went on, 'Come inside, both of you. Marissa, Mum's fretting that you rushed to get here, but she's also bursting to see you. Maybe she'll settle down and rest once she has.'

The combination of protectiveness and residual worry in the man's tone said it all.

The small unit had a living area filled with a two-seater couch and several chairs. A kitchen backed onto the area and there were rooms packed tightly together off a hallway to the right.

Bedroom, bedroom, bathroom, Rick guessed. The laundry room would be at the back behind the kitchen. A woman emerged through an open door and smiled at Marissa. Hugged her briskly and stepped aside. 'Go on and see your mum. A rupture is nasty and it can be very dangerous but your mum's going to be just fine and I'm staying two nights to watch her in any case. It only took me two hours to get here from Tuckwell. I left quickly when your dad phoned.'

Marissa stepped through the door and disappeared. A moment later Rick heard a soft sob quickly stifled, followed by a rush of low words. Marissa's voice and another one—older, soothing and being soothed. He wanted to burst into the room, do something. *Hold Marissa and never let anything upset her again.*

Instead, he stood in the middle of the living room, fists clenched as he forgot all about the two people waiting there, watching him. Then he turned to Marissa's father. 'Your wife truly is well enough to leave the hospital? Marissa was worried.'

'Yes, and Jean will help me keep an eye on her.' Abe examined Rick with shrewd eyes that seemed to have realised something about his guest. Maybe that Rick had eyes only for his daughter.

Rick ran a hand through his hair. 'It's been an uneasy few hours. Far more so for you, I'm sure.'

Abe stared hard at him for a long moment before he spoke again. 'Very true. Now, how long have you and my daughter—'

'Well, it must be time for a cup of tea.' The nurse cleared her throat rather noisily. 'How about I put the kettle on, Abe? I'm sure Tilda would enjoy a cup about now. We probably all could do with one.'

On her way past Rick, she gestured towards one of the squashy cloth-covered lounge chairs. 'Why don't you have a seat? And I'm Jean, Tilda's sister, though I'm sure you've worked that out.

'We can make our way through the introductions properly in a minute and you can tell us how the vintage car festival seems to be shaping up, how many of the cars you saw as you drove in.' She glanced at Abe and her gaze seemed to warn him off launching a more personal inquisition. 'It's one of Milberry's special weekends, you know.'

Rick had given away more of an interest in his borrowed secretary than he should have. At the moment he couldn't raise much concern for the fact. Marissa had needed to get here. Rick had needed to smooth a path for her and he'd go on smoothing one for as long as he felt it was needed.

'I'm afraid I didn't take much notice of the traffic on the way in.' Rick took a seat as ordered and put his hands on his spread knees. He gave himself time to look around this room owned by the people who had raised Marissa. There were photos of her everywhere.

Marissa as a baby, toddler, child and teenager and more recent ones.

'Her hair was always curly.' He murmured the words, took the cup that Jean offered, nodded his thanks. Cleared his throat. 'It is rather noticeable. Her hair.'

'Yes.' Jean slipped into the other room to deliver the tea to Marissa's mum.

That left Rick and Marissa's father. 'There won't be any lingering effects from the illness, I hope?'

The older man rubbed a work-worn hand over his tanned jaw. 'She's exhausted now and they've given her some medication to deal with the after-effects but they say in a few days she won't even know it's happened. I'm just grateful…' He swallowed and took a deep breath. 'Now, if I can just get her to rest properly until she really is all better I'll be satisfied. We could both get a bit of leave from our work—'

'Rick, will you come in and meet Mum before she tries to have a nap?' Marissa asked from the doorway of her mother's room, and Rick rose immediately to his feet.

He caught her hand in his briefly at the door. Then he searched her face and noted the slight redness around her eyes. Asked in a low voice, 'Will she mind me seeing her when she's not a hundred per cent?'

'Probably.' Marissa's smile held relief and gratitude and a wealth of affection for the woman Rick had yet to meet. 'But her curiosity about my boss will overrule that.'

He didn't feel like a boss right now. The expression in Marissa's eyes as she looked at him, the way she'd curled her fingers around his hand—those hadn't seemed very businesslike either.

They stepped into the bedroom together. There were no chairs. It wasn't a hospital room, but the room shared by two people who'd loved each other and lived together for many years. A framed wedding photo hung on the wall at the foot of the bed. Knick-knacks sat cheek by jowl on a dresser with a man's watch and a well-worn hat.

Rick imagined sharing such a room with

Marissa. The idea was alien and stunning all at once. He turned to the woman in the bed. 'I'm very sorry to know you've been unwell, Mrs Warren.'

Marissa stepped past him, went to her mother and caught her hand in hers, pressed it to her face and kissed the back of it before she eased down gently to sit on the bed beside her mum. 'Yes, you're not allowed to pull a stunt like that again, Mum. You scared me silly.'

'I'll try not to.' Tilda Warren shifted slightly in the bed and, though her face bore the marks of the strain and discomfort she'd experienced, she looked enough like Marissa that Rick couldn't help but like her on sight.

She smiled at Rick. 'Thank you for bringing Marissa to us. I won't pretend I'm not glad to see her. The last few hours were a bit frightening and I'm glad to see my girl.'

'And now you're going to rest and hopefully go to sleep.' Marissa fussed a little and then, with obvious reluctance and an equal amount of determination, prepared to leave the room. 'I'll look in on you later, even if you've gone to sleep. Just to be sure…'

'Thank you, love.' Tilda sighed. 'I admit I feel

rather wiped out and I think I probably will sleep, at least for a while. They gave me painkillers. You'll need some dinner, though, and—'

'And we can take care of that by ourselves,' Marissa interrupted with a loving smile, and they left the room together.

The depth of the relief Rick felt surprised him. That Marissa's mother would be okay; that nothing had happened that would cause Marissa a lot of long-term unhappiness.

When Marissa stared rather blankly at the contents of the fridge, he asked if there were any restaurants or take-away food places in the town. 'You've all had a stressful time. Let me at least pick up something for dinner.'

He did that, managing it without stepping on Abe's toes. Abe sat with his wife even after sleep claimed her before he finally emerged and spent some time talking quietly with his daughter while his sister-in-law got up and down at intervals to look in on Marissa's mum.

They spoke in hushed tones of nothing much. Abe asked a little about Rick's business. Jean asked about his roots, and Rick admitted he'd never lived outside the city, that his sisters and nieces were there. His gaze tracked Marissa's every movement. He had a plan for how he might do something for her mother as well…

Mum truly would be okay. Marissa looked in on her one last time and finally started to believe it. As she acknowledged this, some of the things she'd pushed aside in her haste to get here filtered through at last, and she frowned for a whole other set of reasons.

She stood and collected her bag from where she must have dumped it beside a lounge chair when she'd first come into the house. 'You'll be all right through the night, Aunty?'

'Absolutely, and Abe can handle me creeping in and out of the room a few times to see to meds and things tonight.' Jean rose to her feet as well. 'It means turning you out of the spare room, though. There's only a single in there with the sewing machine.'

Marissa glanced towards Rick. He'd also got to his feet and stood watching her. In truth his gaze had rarely left her since they'd arrived, and she felt ridiculously warmed and…comforted by that knowledge. 'If Rick doesn't mind, we'll find a couple of rooms in one of the motels for the night. I'd like to visit Mum again tomorrow morning and then I know we'll have to leave.'

Jean patted her arm. 'Your dad will look after her and she'll stay quieter if there aren't too many people here to distract her from that. You know what she's like. She was already saying she wanted to get out of bed and start organising things.'

They were all on their feet now, and Rick gestured towards the second bedroom in the house. 'Do you keep anything here, Marissa? Maybe you should gather a change of clothes and some nightwear and a toothbrush before we go.'

'You won't get any rooms.' The words came from Abe as he slapped a hand against his thigh. 'I forgot about the impact of the vintage car festival. All the motels are fully booked, or so it said in the paper this morning.'

'And Rick has no spare clothes, not even a toothbrush.' Marissa turned his way. 'I'm sorry. I didn't give that a thought when we left Sydney. I do have a few things here, but you—'

Rick shrugged his broad shoulders. 'I'll make do, and maybe we can go to a motel in a nearby town?'

'The nearest town large enough is mine, and

it's a two-hour drive away.' Jean pointed this out with a frown. 'You'd both be most welcome to stay at my place but it's a long way.'

At that moment a soft knock sounded on the front door. Her father opened it.

It was Mrs Brill from the end of the street, a busy woman with five children and a truck-driver husband. She had a casserole in one hand and a key in the other.

She held out the casserole. 'This is for dinner tomorrow night, and I saw the extra cars outside and wondered about accommodation. I've got the converted garage with a sofa bed that pulls out and a camp-bed I bought at a garage sale for the second room in there.'

'That would be really helpful. We were just wondering how best to work that out.' Jean spoke the words in her brisk, no-nonsense way. She took the casserole and handed it to Marissa, who carried it through to the kitchen.

By the time Marissa returned, matters were decided—Mrs Brill had left to start the short walk back to her home and Rick held the key to the converted garage.

CHAPTER ELEVEN

MARISSA gathered her things into a carryall. Her father bundled some more things in on top for Rick to use and, with a murmured word of thanks, Rick drove them the short distance to the end of the street.

He pulled to a stop before an unpretentious home with a large front garden and larger back garden. Mrs Brill had walked ahead of them and took them straight through to the back, where the garage sat surrounded by a swing set and a collection of children's toys and bikes and other things.

'Thank you. This is very kind.' Marissa managed to choke out the words without looking at Rick at all. Mrs Brill *was* kind, and Marissa appreciated the hospitality. She just couldn't imagine her multi-millionaire boss, with his city central penthouse apartment with all mod cons, here.

'You're welcome, love. You even have your own shower and loo.' Their hostess disappeared with a wave.

Rick unlocked the converted garage, flipped the light switch and they stepped inside.

The room had a square of someone's old carpet slung over a concrete floor, unlined walls covered in dartboards and fishing paraphernalia, and a sofa that converted. A pile of bedding and two bath towels sat waiting on it.

A door to the right opened into a second room.

Marissa bit her lip. 'It's probably not what you're used to, but it was very good of Mrs Brill.'

'It's fine, and it was very generous of her.' Rick set the bag down on the floor and tossed a can of deodorant in on top that he'd taken from the glove compartment of his car.

'I don't know what Dad's put in the bag for you.' For no clear reason, Marissa's face heated and she looked everywhere but into Rick's eyes.

She hadn't thought too much about their accommodation until now, and was realising that it could feel a little awkward for a whole other lot of reasons.

The moment the thought rose so did her consciousness of him.

'Toothbrush, disposable razor, a pair of boxer shorts still in their wrapping, T-shirt, and the ugliest pair of long john style pyjamas I've ever seen.' Rick's tone deepened as he spoke those last words, as his gaze met with hers and held.

'Dad usually wears a T-shirt and boxers to bed. Maybe he wasn't thinking straight.' She spoke the words with a hint of confusion, felt far more as her senses began to respond to Rick's nearness, to the intensity that had risen in his gaze.

'He's your father. He was thinking perfectly.' Rick turned abruptly towards the second room. 'I'd better set up the camp-bed so we can both get some sleep. Mrs Brill said it hasn't been used since she bought it.'

Marissa's face heated even more as she recalled some of Dad's questions to Rick, about his work, his prospects. Surely her father hadn't viewed Rick as a possible boyfriend or something?

You've kissed the man and you are *still attracted to him. Maybe Dad noticed that.*

'You don't have to… I wouldn't want you to think, or feel you need to…'

'You really are tempting when you blush like that.' He spoke the words in a hungry tone of gravel and midnight. 'God knows I'm trying not to notice, Marissa, but I think you know what I am thinking, and for all that those thoughts appear to have me by the throat right now, they can't do either of us any good.'

'You're…you're right. I'll take the camp-bed. It won't be very large and you'll probably only have a sleeping bag for it, and a pillow. No doubt Mrs Brill left a pillow.' The words babbled out of her as they stepped into the second room together. 'See, there's a pillow there.'

'I thought I'd driven you away, you know— lost your approval and good regard when I made the mistake of looking into your working history.' The softening of his tone seemed to sit uneasily with him, yet his gaze revealed how that thought had bothered him.

Rick's jaw clenched as he stared at the pile of canvas and wood and springs and hooks. 'I didn't need to do that, Marissa. I knew it but I went after the information anyway because I felt you were holding something back from me. It's too late to undo it but I want you to know I very much regret the incident.'

'I believe you.' She couldn't raise any anger. Not in the face of his regret, and all he had done for her since.

He's not Michael Unsworth. You can't continue to compare the two. Rick is a far better man in so many ways.

It was a dangerous conclusion, even as she admitted the truth of it. Rick's layers were beginning to make too much sense, appeal too much. She had to remember he still wanted nothing to do with the kind of relationship she hoped one day to find. He didn't want commitment.

Since that seemed to be all she wanted lately, with a side order of Family and Babies and Not Feeling Old When She Turned Thirty thrown in, it would be a very good thing if she could stop being so attracted to her boss.

He drew a breath. 'I'm glad you've forgiven me. Now, let's see about this camp-bed.'

'It looks rather old. So does the sleeping bag.' She eyed both dubiously and returned her gaze to the bed. 'I'm guessing there probably isn't an instruction manual for putting that together.'

Rick glanced at her. One brief, intent, aware glance as the walls of the room seemed to close in on them. He rubbed a hand over the back of his neck. 'I'm sure I can figure it out, and you won't be sleeping on it. I will.'

He tossed the pillow and sleeping bag aside, crouched down and started to assemble the bed. In fact, he had it put together minutes later.

Marissa smiled despite herself. 'I should have known you'd do that with the same precision you do everything.'

With a slight smile he picked up the sleeping bag, unzipped it and laid it flat over the surface of the bed, then leaned down to press the centre with his hand. 'See? It looks quite comfy. I'm sure it'll be fine.'

He turned to reach for the pillow. As he did, the bed snapped down in the middle and up at both ends. Wood crunched and splintered. Springs twanged and bits and pieces flew in all directions.

'What—?' Rick pulled her back, his shoulder turned to protect her from anything that might fly through the air.

Seconds later it was all over, and so was the bed. Marissa stared at the splintered old wood, bits of torn canvas, the sleeping bag tangled within it all, and springs that had irrevocably sprung. 'Oh, my. That was rather dramatic, wasn't it? It made matchsticks out of some of it.'

'Dramatic? The thing could have taken out

your eye. And how I'll explain this to your Mrs Brill—' Rick broke off with a disgusted manly snort of outrage and offence. 'I'm *certain* I put the bed together correctly.'

'Oh, I'm sure you did. It just…cracked under the pressure.' A laugh burst from her. She just couldn't help it. 'Your face! This isn't a corporate implosion, you know.'

'I'll arrange for a new bed to replace it.' He growled the words and kicked one of the larger pieces of wood with his foot. 'Maybe we can get rid of the evidence before morning.'

'That—' Another laugh choked out of her. 'We could bury the evidence in the garden.' Her grin spread. 'Shovels at twenty paces. I won't tell if you don't.'

His brows snapped down and he glared at her and she laughed all the harder until she had to lean over with her arms wrapped around her tummy.

'I don't see anything the least bit amusing about this.' His lips twitched. He kicked another piece of wood out of the way.

A moment later he started to laugh as well. His deep chuckles filled the air.

Marissa grinned at him and sucked up lungfuls

of air and then, to her mortification, tears welled in the backs of her eyes. She blinked them back, turned away so he wouldn't see while she fought for control.

'Hey. It's okay.' Gentle arms came around her, turned her into his chest. 'Your Mum's all right. Your aunt said she'll be almost as good as new tomorrow.'

'How did you know?' The moment he reached for her she'd wrapped her arms around him. Now she lifted her head, gave it a rueful shake even as her body wanted so very much to press to his and never move away. 'I don't know where that came from. I thought I'd settled down after I saw for myself she was okay. And *I'm* fine now, aside from feeling silly again.'

'You could never be silly.' He closed his eyes and kissed the tip of her nose and then he just…held onto her.

She could have stayed there for ever—in his arms, giving and receiving comfort and closeness.

But she wanted more. Her body wanted to meld to his, curves to angles, softness to strength.

'I mustn't…' He murmured the words and set her away from him.

He retrieved the sleeping bag then, and shook it. Splinters of wood rained onto the floor. Many more of them stuck like porcupine quills to the sleeping bag's thin, lumpy lining.

'I'll sleep on the floor.' His voice rumbled the words. 'Why don't you take a shower and I'll make up the other bed for you before I wash? You'll want to be up early in the morning to see your mum again.'

'Thanks.' Their prosaic words did nothing to cover the tension that had risen between them. 'I…I guess I will have a quick shower.' She'd raided the room at the unit for a pair of comfy pyjama bottoms she'd had about a hundred years, a spaghetti-strap stretchy top and loose jumper and old jeans and a shirt to wear for tomorrow, toiletries and spare panties.

Marissa bundled up what she needed and disappeared into the bathroom that had obviously been somebody's DIY project. She couldn't let Rick sleep on the floor with splinters sticking all through that sleeping bag, but she needed to pull herself together a little before they had that discussion.

Rick showered while she sent text messages to Dani and Grace and let them know that Mum was going to be okay, though she planned to keep a closer eye on her parents' health from now on!

When Rick came out of the bathroom, Marissa was already in the bed, the jumper discarded, and had brought the pillow from the other room and placed it beside hers. Action seemed the best way to address the issue.

Rick's gaze roved over her face and shoulders and snapped back to her eyes. 'Is this a good idea?'

She'd glanced at him, just once, before she too focused her attention solely on *his* face. That single moment had revealed his broad tanned chest, narrow hips and thighs encased in dark boxers, long bare legs. 'We have to be sensible.'

The comment referred to him sleeping in the bed, not on the floor, but could have referred equally to her runaway thoughts right now. She wanted Rick to climb into the bed, wrap his arms around her and make love to her. She wanted it with her senses, and with deeper emotions. She wanted it for herself, not only because her hormones were giving her trouble. She was afraid to look deeper into all the other reasons she wanted it.

'I'll use the sleeping bag. I shook it out.' He said the words even as his gaze devoured her and tenderness formed in that gaze. 'If not on the floor, then I'll sleep on top of the bedcovers.'

'The sleeping bag is prickled right through with splinters still. I checked.' That tenderness somehow helped her to regain some of her equilibrium. She gestured as calmly as she could to the space beside her. 'It's roomy enough. We'll stick to our sides. I just want to sleep and forget the stress of worrying about Mum during that trip.'

It was the right thing to say.

He relaxed a little at last, murmured, 'I guess if there's no choice, there's no choice.' He turned the light off, plunged the room into darkness and she heard him pad across the carpeted floor towards her.

One last bout of nerves got her then.

'You didn't wear Dad's pyjamas. Not that you should have. No doubt you thought they were quite hideous and it's not as though he should try to intimidate you or imply anything about the two of us or try to circumvent certain behaviour.' Each word tumbled after the other. 'Not that we intend to indulge in such behaviour.'

The bed dipped as he sat on the edge.

'I…er…I don't usually sleep in any… No, I didn't wear the pyjamas.' A rustling sound followed as he settled into the bed right beside her. All that naked skin on his upper torso and…

His weight rolled her into the middle. Their bodies brushed before she quickly pulled herself back to her side.

'Sorry.'

'My fault.' He inhaled. Stilled. Finally murmured into the darkness, 'You smell the same. Of flowers.'

They were facing each other in the darkness. She knew it from the direction of his words and she thrilled to that small knowledge even when she shouldn't have.

'I…er…yes. The perfume…I keep some of the perfume in my bag.' If she leaned forward a little, would they touch? Would he wrap his arms around her and kiss her?

Don't think about it, Marissa. You're being sensible now, remember?

'I hope the smell isn't bothering you.'

'No.' His voice dipped to a low, dark tone. 'It's not bothering me.'

For a moment, silence reigned and then he said painfully, 'I don't want to hurt you. What your parents have with each other, what you deserve to have, I can't go there. Relationships for me...don't go there. Because of my family, the example of my father. I'm not assuming, or suggesting anything...'

'It's fine. It's always best to say what you're thinking, make it all clear.' And he had, and it was hard to hear it—hard when they lay so close together and her body longed for the touch of his.

A part of her still wanted his touch now, and a part of her wondered if it would be so bad. If she gave in to her desire for him, even though there could be no future in it. Just one time, to make love with him—with due care and responsibility—so she could at least have that experience, that memory of him.

But that was all it would be, because he wasn't Mr Right For Her. All else aside, he didn't match her criteria. He was still Mr Corporate. 'Um... well...we should go to sleep.'

'Yes. We definitely should sleep.' Rick wanted Marissa so much he ached all over from it. The way she'd been with her parents this evening had caught at something inside him, had deepened his feelings towards her in ways he hadn't been able to fathom or control. It was why he'd pushed her away with his words.

'*You* should try to sleep, anyway.' He doubted he would do the same with her so close.

His leg brushed against hers as he repositioned himself in the bed and he registered a long length of flannelette.

The ugliest and most unromantic nightwear in the world for women. Wasn't that what they said? She had apparently covered herself from belly to ankle in the stuff. Her shoulders had been bare, with just a thin strap indicating some kind of fitted top.

Images of running his hands over her legs and thighs over that thick cloth invaded his brain anyway. He felt far from repelled right now.

He forced his attention to other things. To the reason they'd come here. Maybe, if he focused on that, he would find the control and distance he needed to endure this night without reaching for her, without reaching for all he wanted *from* her and *with* her that he must not take. 'Are you okay now, Marissa? About your mother?'

'Yes. I cross-questioned her about what had happened until she probably wanted me to shut up, but I needed to know she truly would be all right.' Marissa's breath caressed his face as she sighed into the darkness.

Did she realise exactly how close they were? That their heads were turned intimately towards each other?

'Mum said I didn't need to rush here, that she didn't expect that.'

'She wanted to see you, though. Your father told me he was glad you'd come so quickly.' *Her* family held a strong bond for each other.

He didn't have that with his parents. And he didn't know *how* to have it with a woman. Marissa was right to want someone who didn't come with a bunch of complications attached.

You could figure it out. You could risk it.

He stilled, and then he clamped down on the thoughts and an unexpected well of anger towards his father rose up instead.

No. Rick would never risk short-changing a family the way Dad had, and that meant not risking his own family, period.

'Mum was worried about missing shifts at the newsagent's. Silly thing.' Marissa fell silent and Rick thought she might finally try to go to sleep, or at least pretend to, as he would.

Then she spoke again in a low tone of admission. 'It scared me to see Mum vulnerable. My parents have always been strong and I've never thought about losing them. I should do more to show how much I appreciate them.'

'What would you do? They seem happy, and proud of you. I looked at the pictures of you in their living room.' Had looked—had wanted to touch each one. Had wondered if she had a child, would it have her hair? Those expressive brown eyes?

'Some of those pictures are awful.' Despite the words, a smile filled her tone.

He'd planned to bring this up in the morning, but, 'What about sending your parents on a holiday? I've done it for my sisters occasionally.' He drew a breath, wished he could see her face to know if she would allow him to do this for her, to give her this.

He'd been thinking of it since Abe had said he wished he could ensure his wife rested properly. 'I have a holiday home on the Queensland coast that's vacant right now, just sitting there doing nothing. They could spend a week there. Your father mentioned he'd like to take her away, that they could both get holiday. He wants to make sure she spends proper time resting up. In truth, I'd appreciate having someone there to check the place is being looked after properly under the caretaking arrangements I've made for it.'

In the face of her silence, because he didn't know what she was thinking, he added, 'It's easy to reach. They could fly direct from the nearest airport.' He considered trying to sell her on the local attractions. Made himself stop speaking and wait for her answer.

'I'm sure they'd love it. I'll talk to Dad and I'll buy them plane tickets.' Her hand reached through the darkness, found his upper arm and tracked down it until she found his hand and gripped it. 'Thank you for thinking of it, Rick. That will be perfect for them, and it's very generous of you.'

He couldn't prevent himself from lifting their joined hands, kissing her fingers, pressing that hand against his chest and drawing a deep breath as he held it there. 'You're welcome. I'm happy to do it, and they'll be helping me at the same time.'

His heart had started to thump. Just because he had her hand pressed to his chest. Just because…he wanted her so very much.

'Try to sleep.' He rasped the words past an in-explicable ache in his throat, releasing his grip on her hand one finger at a time because he couldn't manage more. 'I traded cellphone numbers with your father and obviously they have yours. If they need you they'll call, but I don't think that'll happen, and your mum will probably be happier if you seem well-rested when she sees you tomorrow.'

'Goodnight, Rick.' Marissa didn't expect to sleep. She lay there absorbing the slight musty smell of the room and Rick's far nicer scent of soap and deodorant and warm man beside her. Thought about her mum and dad and what Rick had done for her today, and about his family and his limitations…

How ironic that she now wanted Mr Tall, Dark and Aggressive About Success and he'd made it clear he could never be right for her.

Rick woke to the tenderest feeling deep inside, and realised he had Marissa clutched in his arms like the most precious of bundles. His face was pressed into her hair and her softness seemed to melt into him.

His arms locked and for a long, still moment he couldn't let go as his heart began to hammer and emotion swamped him. A cold sweat broke out on his brow.

'Rick,' she murmured. Her eyelids fluttered

up to reveal sleepy eyes and something deep inside him shifted and parted and tried very hard to let her in.

Panic welled inside him and he eased his hold on her and moved away.

'Is it morning?' Her lips were soft, so kissable, her face flushed from sleep.

Heat flared in his body then, but even that couldn't fully wipe out his earlier feelings of…what?

He didn't know, only felt the ache still, that had seemed to insist that if he held her close enough he could somehow assuage that emptiness.

'It's early, but yes, it's morning.' He rolled to the side of the bed, swung his legs over and sat with his back to her. Tried for coherence—he who always had control of himself and now felt he had very little of any. 'We should take our showers. Maybe once we're both through it'll be a reasonable enough time to visit your mother. I'll leave a cheque for Mrs Brill to pay for the broken bed in the other room.'

Rick retrieved his clothes from the carryall and shut himself in the bathroom. Perhaps a blast of cold water would straighten out the confusion of his mind—and settle his senses!

CHAPTER TWELVE

'IT'S good that your mother seemed much better this morning, and I'm glad she and your father let us talk them into taking that holiday.' Rick's hands tightened slightly around the steering wheel as he spoke. 'You're happy with how long you stayed, the amount of time you had with her?'

He wore her father's T-shirt loose over his suit trousers and looked a little rumpled and delicious and appealing and, beneath that, tense. He'd been that way since they'd woken this morning with their arms around each other.

In that first moment, before she'd remembered his words of warning to her last night, Marissa had hoped he might kiss her. The desire had been there in his gaze, but with other emotions she hadn't fully understood. He'd seemed almost uncertain for a moment, somehow shocked and uneasy at the same time.

After that he'd withdrawn physically from holding her. She'd remembered why that was the only sensible course of action. He still seemed withdrawn.

Except when your eyes meet because, in the first instant when that happens, you have all his attention and there's warmth amongst that attention. Warmth and desire and...

No. There was no *and*—there couldn't be. She had to keep her imagination and all the hopes it wanted to raise under control.

'I hope you didn't mind hanging around for hours again. I would have liked to stay longer but it will be easier for Dad to get Mum to rest if I'm not there, and then, when she's recovered enough, he'll whip her away for that week at the beach. They'll probably go on Tuesday, if she continues to feel better.' Perhaps, if they discussed this kind of thing, he would eventually relax?

And you, Marissa?

She admitted she had formed a bond inside herself to him somehow in the past day and night, despite everything. To wake held in his arms had felt safe and right and wonderful. It had seemed to tell her in physical action of a great deal of his care and she had wanted—

She'd wanted to give that care back to him in the same way, and that knowledge terrified her because Rick had simply been holding her. If he'd felt something, perhaps it was empathy because she'd been afraid for her mum. And Marissa couldn't let herself feel a great deal more for him.

You're sure you don't already feel those things?

Uneasy, she shifted in her seat. These feelings surpassed even the confusing and disconcerting ones of longing for a baby, of feeling so broody and so resistant to the idea of turning thirty and being alone.

'I'm just pleased Mum seems so much better. And I really do appreciate what you did to take me to her.'

'I hope she doesn't go through anything like that again.' He drew out to overtake a slow-moving truck, and smoothly returned them to their lane.

They'd left Milberry after brunch at Mum and Dad's unit. Marissa had missed her computer access this morning. She'd come to rely on checking in for instant chat messages from Grace and Dani. How would she get on now with her plan to find Mr Right on the dating site when her thoughts centred so much on Mr Couldn't Be Right?

What would Dani and Grace think of this morning's events?

Nothing, because I'm not going to tell them. Marissa focused her stare out of the window without really looking at anything they passed. Grace and Dani were her friends. They meant a lot to her and she *liked* confiding in them but she had to sort these feelings out about Rick for herself.

Sort them and then leave them behind. Her chest hurt at the thought but she wasn't falling for him. She liked him, appreciated him.

He was not someone she could love.

And you, Marissa? You're completely straightforward? You're not carrying around any emotional complications?

She didn't have any family troubles. And she refused to consider any memories of fiancé troubles. She was over all that.

As he drew his car to a stop outside Marissa's apartment building, weariness tugged at Rick. He turned his head, noted the shadows beneath Marissa's eyes. 'Let's see you up to your place.'

'Come up with me.' Marissa made the request in a soft tone edged with concern. 'I want you to drink some coffee before you go any further. It's been a big weekend and…we woke very early this morning.'

Even this obscure reference to those moments in a borrowed garage tugged at him. At his senses, he assured himself. Only in that way. He wanted her still. Enough that he couldn't get the thought of making love with her out of his mind.

This was true, but he also couldn't get the thought of *holding* her out of his mind. Holding her and never letting go. He'd warned her off, but now *he* didn't want to be warned off, even though that was the only option for Stephen Morgan's son. Was this what Faith had meant and what he'd said he wouldn't do? Was he poised on the edge of that dive into emotional oblivion?

If so, he didn't like the feeling, and he could not allow himself to take that leap. Even the thought of that being a possibility terrified him.

Just as his father must have felt terrified, and had thus drawn back?

It wasn't the same.

Maybe it was exactly the same. Did that even

matter? His instinct told him he mustn't—couldn't—want Marissa so deeply, so for her sake. Yes, for her sake he had to shut those feelings down.

'Coffee's ready. It's only instant, I'm afraid, but I didn't want you to have to wait too long for it.' Marissa carried the drinks into her small living room, only to find Rick sprawled out on her sofa, his chin on his chest. Spiky lashes formed crescents on strong male cheeks. He'd lain right back so his feet dangled off the end of the third cushion. He was fast asleep.

He looked younger, exhausted, and somehow vulnerable this way. Her heart ached as she stared at him. Feelings she hadn't meant to allow welled inside her, wanted to be set free.

How could this one man have found his way into such hidden parts of her so easily and so quickly? The mega-boss man. She had judged him by Michael's standards when she shouldn't have. Rick cared for his sisters and his nieces, was capable of acts of kindness.

He had also stepped outside her perception of acceptable boundaries when he'd investigated her; he wasn't right for Marissa.

Because he didn't have enough to give to a relationship. Because he would always have a ruthless edge—the part of him that had made him a success in business, even if he'd gone about achieving that success by more acceptable means than Michael. What if he turned that edge on her? Hurt her with it, as Michael had hurt her?

Marissa set aside the coffee, covered Rick with her one and only patchwork quilt from her handicraft phase and went into her bedroom with her laptop computer. It was time to sign onto Blinddatebrides.com and do something proactive about the *real* future she needed to seek.

To: Englishcrumpet, Sanfrandani
From Kangagirl
Did you know you can tell how old a woman is by what happens when she pinches the skin of the back of her hand between her fingers?

From: Englishcrumpet
Thanks a lot, Marissa. Now I feel really depressed.

From: Sanfrandani
I don't get it. Is that one of those English/Australian jokes?

From: Kangagirl
If the skin goes back quickly, you're not old.

From: Englishcrumpet
Sigh.

From: Sanfrandani
Oh. Well, my skin seems okay, and… er…duty calls. I have to say goodbye for now. TTYL.
Sanfrandani has signed out.

From: Englishcrumpet
What's going on, Marissa? I'm getting the same vibe I get when Daisy is holding something back from me.

From: Kangagirl
It's nothing. Actually, it's something. I thought I could sign on to Blinddatebrides.com and find Mr Nice, Ordinary and Unthreatening.

I thought I could vet candidates and find one to match my criteria and magically make us fall in love with each other or something. That I could keep myself safe from getting hurt that way. My thirtieth birthday is getting closer and I don't want to get old, I'm starting to wonder if I'm scared I'll never have a chance to have a baby, and I think—I think I might have sort of half slightly started to fall for my boss.

From: Englishcrumpet
Oh, Marissa.

From: Kangagirl
I don't know—maybe I should quit my Blinddatebrides subscription. I'm not sure I can keep looking for a man on the site any more.

From: Englishcrumpet
You must have had an exhausting time of it. Why don't you have a rest and worry about your Blinddatebrides plans and all the rest of this later? Maybe this will all

look better when you're not so tired. One thing I know is Dani and I won't want to lose your friendship!

From: Kangagirl
I don't think I could cope with losing either of you. I am tired. I think I'll close my eyes for a little while. Over and out for now from Australia.

'I phoned Mum earlier. I thought she might have wanted to hear how Russell was doing,' Faith said to Rick as she walked with him to his car.

It was mid-afternoon on Sunday. Julia was taking a nap inside Faith and Russell's house, and Rick had just eaten lunch with his sister.

'Marissa said it must be hard for you, having Russell away.' The comment simply came out of him, in the same way so many thoughts of Marissa got past his defences.

And yesterday Rick had fallen asleep on Marissa's couch, only to wake hours later and discover her asleep on her bed, her laptop in power saver mode beside her.

Rick had wanted to kiss her awake and make love to her. More than he'd wanted anything in a long time. He'd wavered, had reached for her, but then he'd touched the laptop control pad and a website had shown on the screen.

Blinddatebrides.com. We pride ourselves on our success stories.

There were pictures of brides and grooms smiling into each other's eyes as though they'd found the whole world there. Marissa had been logged in. There'd been an IM chat still sitting in the corner of the screen. He hadn't read it, but it was clear she was a member of the site. Quite possibly the friends she'd mentioned, Grace and Dani, were also on the site.

Rick had walked away and kept walking because that was the right thing to do. The only thing he was able to do. He wished he could stop thinking about her, but that didn't seem to be possible, no matter how much he wanted it.

'She seems really nice, Rick.' His sister touched his arm. 'Why don't you—?'

'That won't happen for me.' The words were harsher than he intended. 'I'm sorry, but you know that's not in my plans.'

'I know you like to tell people you're too old and set in your ways and that the company owns you and any other excuse that feels reasonable at the time.' Faith spoke the words in a low tone. 'I don't think it's the truth. You don't want to be like our father, so you hold yourself back.'

Rick chopped a hand through the air. 'I don't want this conversation with you.'

'Well, too bad, because maybe it's time we had it!' She drew a harsh breath. 'Do you think I don't see what he's like, Rick? Do you think it doesn't bother me every day to know our father treats you and me and my husband and my daughter better than he does Darla or Kirrilea simply because Darla had the bad luck to do something that made him uncomfortable, that put pressure on him which he refused to face up to?'

'He loves everyone in the family.' But their father only loved to a degree, didn't he? It might seem as though Stephen had perfectly normal feelings towards some of his children, his grand-children, but the reality was that it seemed that way because they hadn't pushed him outside his emotional comfort zone. 'If it came down to it, he'd ignore all our needs…'

'Of course he would.' Faith swung to face him. 'If he knew Russell came home from active duty the last two times and cried in my arms for hours, he'd cringe away from it. When Julia gets older and starts to test her boundaries like Kirri's doing now he'll draw back from her too, and the thought of that kills me. If I decided to do something to totally shake him up—'

'That's enough.' For the first time in his life, Rick shut his sister up. 'This conversation is finished. Just leave it, all right?'

Faith's expression froze and then she reached past him to yank his car door open. 'Maybe I've been wrong to believe you're better. To think you could have something with a woman like Marissa. Maybe it's best if you don't.' She stepped back. 'You acted just like him right now.'

Rick drove half a kilometre down the road before he pulled over and used his mobile to phone Faith's house. 'I'm sorry. I didn't mean any of that.'

'I didn't either! I had the phone in my hand to ring you.' Her breath shook as she inhaled. 'You're not like him, Rick. I should never have said it. You've always been there for Darla and me, and our daughters. You're the complete opposite of Dad. Please don't ever believe otherwise.'

Rick reassured his sister and ended the call. But Faith's initial words had been right. He was *exactly* like Stephen Morgan. He'd already proved it once before and left a woman broken-hearted.

CHAPTER THIRTEEN

'I WOULD have taken you out, Darla.' Rick needed to pull his head together, to figure out why he'd lost control when he'd talked with Faith.

Well, Marissa didn't want him anyway, so why was he worrying about it?

Because Marissa is the reason you became so upset?

And, instead of working out anything, he was hosting a family gathering.

His sister toasted him with the gourmet sandwich in her hand and shook her head. 'I didn't want you to take me out. Not this time. This mightn't be anything amazing, but the celebration is on my tab and I want it that way.'

'It's all great.' He meant that. He just hoped she got what she needed from this.

Because Darla had invited them all, and Kirri was at her side and Stephen stood in the corner making polite noises and Rick was so tense he thought he might lose it if anything went wrong for his sister today.

'The sandwiches are fabulous, Darla. Do you mind if I ask which caterer you used?' Marissa asked from beside him.

From the moment Darla had phoned to ask if they could do this today, Marissa had got right behind his sister's plans.

Right now, she couldn't have said anything better if she'd known. Darla grinned and Kirrilea ducked her head with a pleased flush.

Marissa's eyes widened and she laid her hand on his niece's arm. 'It was you? I'm so impressed. Will you tell me what the combination is that has sun-dried tomatoes and cottage cheese and that delicious tangy flavour?'

She'd hit it off with his sisters beautifully—liked Darla on an instinctive level that showed in every word she spoke to her, made Kirri feel great and enjoyed Julia's childish chatter.

If the knowledge of that made Rick possessive about her, maybe he was. If each time he looked at her he wanted to drag her out of there and to the nearest bed and hold her and make love to her, that fact didn't seem any easier to change either.

Rick's mouth tightened and, since there was one thing he *could* do right now that would be utterly appropriate, he forced himself to leave Marissa's side and went round the room charging glasses, moving back to stand beside his sister.

He turned to face Darla and cleared his throat. 'I think a speech is in order. Particularly as you and Kirri have spoiled us all so nicely with food and drink.'

His free hand reached for Darla's. 'You've come a long way from the part-time real estate receptionist who took rental payments over the counter three days a week. You've worked your way up through the ranks and your promotion is well deserved.

'I'm even more proud of what a fabulous parent you are to a very special, wonderful daughter.' The words of pride and love poured out of him and somehow eased him. 'I love you, Darla. I couldn't be more proud of you in all the ways there are.'

'Thank you, Rick. Those words mean the world to me.' Darla smiled through suddenly bright eyes as a still silence descended over the room.

Marissa felt the thrum of heartache mixed with the deep emotion between sister and brother.

So much hurt, and now that she'd observed Stephen Morgan in action, she believed she understood. Rick's father was a pleasant man. He cared for his family. That was quite clear. But he wanted to care only on his terms. Any time things drifted to any kind of emotional ground, he closed himself off from it.

Even in the simple act of his youngest grand-daughter running to him for a cuddle. He had patted her head but he hadn't picked her up. That meting out of a measured amount of affection was so sad, and how difficult he'd made it for his family.

She smiled at Darla with determined good cheer. 'Congratulations. I hope the job promotion is all you want it to be.'

Faith hugged her sister and got a bit tearful. Hugged Rick and got equally tearful.

Rick's mother gave her daughter a peck on the cheek and a smile, and their father cleared his throat and declared it must be time they all left. It was only a brief lunch, after all. He'd reached the door, his wife close behind him, when Darla's mouth firmed and she reclaimed Rick's hand.

'That lovely speech deserves one in return, and in fact I chose to do this here because I wanted to say a few words and I felt this was the right place for them.' She turned her gaze to Rick and her heart was in her eyes so clearly that Marissa caught her breath.

Their parents hesitated in the doorway, but Darla didn't seem to care whether they stayed or left.

Rick started to shake his head, but Darla simply set a jaw very like her brother's and went on.

'Without you, Rick, without your financial support and your encouragement and your unconditional love, I don't know if I could have done any of this.' She swallowed hard. 'You were there when my beautiful girl was born. You'd have come into the labour suite if I'd let you. Instead, they told me you paced non-stop outside until it was over.'

Her gaze skimmed her daughter's down-bent head and returned to her brother. 'Thanks to your financial support, I could be at home with my baby and eventually get my career and my finances on track.'

Rick's Adam's apple bobbed. 'I did very little—'

'You helped me get where I am today, and you helped me know I didn't have to be scared or feel alone or deserted.' Darla's voice cracked. 'You loved my daughter from the day she was born and you've loved me from the day I was born, and I love you and I just…need to say that today.'

She hugged her brother and Rick held her in a tight embrace. His shoulders were taut, his eyes closed as though against such pain. Love for his sister filled every plane and angle of his face.

Marissa took a step towards them before she could stop herself. She needed to hold Rick. To assure him he'd done enough for his sister, that he could…love?

But they drew apart then and after a moment Kirrilea stuck her arm through her mum's and glanced beyond her to the couple near the door.

Her eyes were far too mature for her face as she said, 'Grandad, you probably have golf or something, so don't feel you and Grandma have to stay. We're fine here.'

The older couple left with brief farewells, acting as though nothing were amiss and there'd been no outpouring of emotion in the room just moments before. As though they hadn't been dismissed, if politely. As though they weren't lacking—

'Darla—'

'Don't worry about it, Rick.' Darla squeezed her daughter's shoulders. 'Wise heads on young shoulders, huh? I think we're really okay here. This was a good thing. It was. And it's time for us to head out.'

It was time for Marissa to remember, too, that Rick being able to love his sisters didn't mean he could commit his heart elsewhere. Why was she even thinking this, anyway? *Her* heart was far from involved.

A few minutes later, everyone had left.

'It's time to get back to work.' Rick's preoccupation was clear as he murmured the words, later on, back at the office, but he settled behind his desk and drew a folder of reading material in front of him.

Marissa might even have managed to set aside her reactions and thoughts about him if she hadn't stepped into his office to leave some letters for signature and seen that he'd tacked the laminate of his niece to the wall by his window where it competed with the view of the harbour.

Where he would look at it at least a hundred times a day.

And she admitted it. She wanted to ask a thousand questions and tell him she understood so much more about him now and she wanted him to see all he had inside to give. All he had already given.

Rick had dropped everything to rush her to her mother, but he'd also done all he could to allow Tom a comfortable and worry-free recovery. He had been *kind*. That wasn't the same as a romantic commitment.

Marissa got down to work. She wished she could shut her thoughts down altogether.

'Our Hong Kong businessmen called while you were in the filing room,' Rick said from the doorway of his office half an hour later. He looked rumpled and somehow determined and resigned and intense all at once. 'Tom phoned minutes before them.' His voice turned to a harsh, low rumble. 'He'll be back in the office on Wednesday.'

'That's two days away. I thought he was taking longer.' The whispered words fell from her lips as the shock of that knowledge passed through her. Just two more days and she would cease to see Rick all day every day, work closely with him. Would cease to feel a close part of his life, even if that closeness was only in her…heart?

In her thoughts, in the fact that they had drawn together out of necessity for a short time! Marissa stiffened her spine and tried hard to hide her shock and the dismay she didn't want to admit.

'Well, that's great. Tom must feel a lot better. I'll do my best to leave everything in good order for him, and Gordon is due back on Monday, anyway. I'd been wondering how that would work out.'

Rick ran his fingers through his hair. 'Yes. It will be convenient for…everyone.'

He would be rid of her, wouldn't have to fight his attraction to her any more. Wasn't that what he had wanted from the start? To *not* want her?

'We leave for Hong Kong tomorrow after lunch.' His jaw clenched. 'It will be a two-night stay. They'll tell us with due formality they've chosen to do business with us and, though they could have done that over the phone or with a contract in the mail, it's due process for them, and important we acknowledge the gesture and respond as they expect.'

'And, because I participated in the initial

dealings here, they want me along?' Did *Rick* want her presence there, or did he wish he didn't have to take her with him? 'I've never visited Hong Kong and, though my passport is current, I can invent a reason not to attend if you don't want—'

'I want you to come.' His gaze touched over her hair, each facial feature, dwelt on her mouth and came back to her eyes. 'I'd like to show you some of the sights, take you shopping.'

He wanted to give her a last huzzah before it all ended? The knowledge somehow hurt and wrapped around her heart, all at once.

Marissa tipped up her chin. 'I'd like the chance to visit Hong Kong, see a few of the sights and my presence is expected. I don't want to let the businessmen down.'

It seemed business was all they had left now.

Rick sent Marissa to bed straight off the plane the first night in Hong Kong. He knocked on her hotel room door the next morning and realised how much he wanted this time with her.

His plans, his way of showing her—what? A good time in a place she'd never visited before? So he could say goodbye this way and not look back afterwards? His body burned with the need to be near hers. His emotions burned for her in ways he had never expected or experienced.

Something had happened that day when Darla had brought their family's relationships to the fore and Kirri had dealt with her grandfather with a teenage combination of kindness and something close to pity. Rick had felt as though, finally, an issue that had hovered over all of them had been addressed.

Quietly and without any particular fanfare, but that exchange with his sister had loosened something tight way down inside him.

Rick hadn't realised how the situation had festered, even while he'd believed he had pushed it all aside.

But you're still like your father.

He didn't want to be like Stephen, but he'd already proved he was. Marissa didn't deserve that. She needed someone tender, gentle, and completely committed to her. Someone who would *know* his ability to meet all her needs.

'Good morning. These rooms are great. I have the most amazing view of Victoria Harbour and the city.' Marissa stood framed in the doorway of her room.

A fierce determination seized him. For today

he planned to spoil her and indulge her and enjoy her. He would have *that much*.

And then she could go back to Gordon's office and to her search for a man?

Her gaze rushed over him like a warm breath and ducked away again, and all his senses fired to life despite himself. No. He still didn't want her searching for a man, but he chose to push that thought away for now.

'All the colour and activity I glimpsed last night really is as stunning as I thought.' She touched her hair self-consciously, smoothed her hands over cream trousers, and skimmed the buttons of her brown long-sleeved blouse.

Nervous. She was nervous.

You could try speaking instead of standing here eating her up with your eyes.

She'd said the view was stunning.

'It is a great view.' But he meant the one in front of him right now. 'We have a spending budget for today,' he ventured, and wondered if she'd believe him if he said their businessmen hosts had provided it.

'Work-related expenditure? Tax deductibles?' She raised a hand to her hair again and he wished he could pull the ribbon from it and let it loose.

Instead, he took her arm, led her away from the room. 'Not all of it, no, but I'll be very disappointed if you don't join me and enjoy the day. We're going to visit a temple, see an outdoor Chinese opera, shop, ride in a rickshaw.'

'It sounds magical.' Did her voice hold a touch of wistfulness?

Rick forced a smile. 'We don't meet our hosts until this evening. They've planned a pre-dinner cocktail cruise on a junk so we can see the light show. The pace here is frenetic and the volume of people can take you by surprise so stay close to me and tell me if you need a time-out if I don't create one for you soon enough, okay?'

Rick took Marissa through all the things he'd promised. A wiry man pedalled them along the street in a rickshaw with a gaily coloured top. When they'd taken in the awe of a Buddhist temple and the outdoor opera and so much bustling activity in the markets that Marissa felt dizzy with it, Rick hustled her into an opulent boutique hotel restaurant tucked away between towering buildings.

'This afternoon we'll shop.' He made the announcement as they ate food he'd chosen from a confusingly long list of Cantonese dishes—small servings of prawn and pork dumpling, steamed bean curd with salted fish sauce and other stunningly flavoured foods they interspersed with sips of tea.

'I've already bought some things.' She gestured to the goodies bundled at their feet. 'For Mum and Dad.'

'This afternoon I want you to buy for yourself. Pretty things. Whatever takes your fancy.' He lowered his eyes as though he couldn't quite meet hers as he admitted this.

The desire to burrow her fingers through the hair at his nape rushed through her. When their eyes locked she saw a sharp ache in him before he blinked it away.

'Rick…' She wanted him to open himself to her, to let her in totally. 'I can't let you buy me—'

'Yes. You can. If you don't, I'll only add the money to your pay.' His stare compelled her, almost implored her. 'Don't think too much, Marissa. Just agree. It would please me.'

Her hand tightened in her lap. How could she deny him when he asked her this way?

When he seemed to need this so much?

Just as he'd needed Darla to let him do something to help make her attempt at a business promotion successful. No. Not like that, because he *loved* Darla. This was *kindness*, nothing more.

'Then I guess we really are going shopping.'

They finished their meal and he ushered her to her feet. He arranged for their packages to be returned to their hotel for them, and he took her shopping.

Patiently and with absolute pleasure as she delighted herself in the most sumptuous retail experience she would perhaps encounter in her life. She wouldn't spend much. Just one or two things to please them both.

'What about this shop?' Rick drew her attention to a store full of exquisite silk garments and she knew she wouldn't be able to walk out of the place empty-handed. She stopped short. 'Oh, no.'

'Yes. Pick something to wear tonight. There must an outfit here you'd like.' He turned her to the displays of clothing.

She found the dress almost straight away. A simple cream sheath with a lovely watermark effect in the fabric. It was sleeveless, with a high traditional collar and exquisitely fitted bodice covered in tiny hand-sewn pearls. Her fingers reached for it, stopped just shy of touching as she imagined how much it might cost.

'Try it on,' he growled before he spoke in Cantonese to the shop assistant nearest them.

Moments later, tucked into the privacy of a changing room, Marissa lifted her arms and allowed the dress to glide over her head and settle against her curves.

The rustle of the fabric was almost sinful— whisper-soft and sleek—and the dress fitted as though made for her. She had to have it, wanted to wear it. For him.

No. Because it was beautiful, lovely.

While Marissa tried the dress on, Rick bought a shawl to go with it and arranged for it to be delivered to the hotel. A cream and brown confection that reminded him of her skin and her hair and her deep, expressive eyes.

When she emerged from the changing room with her face flushed a delicate pink and the dress clutched carefully in her hands, a surge of possessive heat rose inside him. He wanted to lavish gifts on her for the rest of his days, dress her in beautiful things and then strip those things away from her body and make love to her slowly and thoroughly and never have to stop.

And afterwards he wanted to hold her, cradled in his arms. None of which could ever happen.

'Did it fit?' Even to his ears, his voice was low and rough, sensual and far too intense. He'd brought her here to say goodbye, but he'd intended to control that leave-taking, not have to fight himself all the way.

'Yes. Yes, it fitted.' She swallowed, looked as though she didn't know whether to run or come closer.

It was too much. His fingers reached for her wrist and the warmth of her soft skin. He circled the fragile bones and inhaled slowly. Her pulse fluttered beneath his thumb.

'The…er…the shoes I've packed will go nicely with the dress.' She lifted her other hand, dropped it before she touched him. 'And it really is—'

'Beautiful.' But not as beautiful as Marissa. He released her reluctantly, completed the transaction for her and then rubbed a hand over the back of his neck.

'There's a jewellery store beside this one. I'd like to pick up something for my sisters and nieces.' And he would like to buy Marissa all kinds of necklaces and bracelets.

'I might like a scarf or something from here before I go.' She glanced around her. 'Out of my own money. I'll meet you in the jewellery store in a few minutes.'

Dismissed again, very nicely, and despite himself he couldn't help the tug of a smile as he remembered other times she had dispatched him.

Rick left her to it.

His body tingled with awareness as he walked out of the store, and with an odd ache because he didn't like separating from her. He could say it was because he needed her close for her sake. She couldn't speak the language. But he practised his Cantonese to keep the skills. It often wasn't needed, and she was more than capable of keeping herself safe without him.

The jewellery store was top end, and had every conceivable gift item. Rick's gaze shifted to the display of engagement rings. What kind of ring had Michael Unsworth given Marissa, if any?

His brows drew down. At the same time his gaze landed on a ring that would be perfect for her. A rare amber stone set against rich brown tiger's eye and surrounded by diamonds. It would match her eyes and hair. He wanted to buy it for her. Dear God, he wanted to—

Rick turned away from the display with a stifled sound of shock and rejection and…disbelief.

And then she was there beside him, a small store bag clutched to her side with the top pinched tightly together so there was no chance he would glimpse inside it.

Her gaze went to the displays of jewellery, though not the engagement rings. 'I wonder if I could find something for Dani and Grace. I think it's just as well we'll need to leave here soon. This sort of retail therapy is rather addictive.' She glanced up at him then, and her face stilled. 'Are you—?'

'I'm fine. I'll…help you look.'

She cast one or two uncertain glances his way as they browsed, but eventually he must have pulled himself together enough that she stopped wondering what was wrong with him.

Rick didn't know the answer to that. He helped her choose gifts for her friends and, when he purchased items for his sisters and nieces and mother, added a jewelled headband for Marissa. He was under control again. He couldn't be anything else, could he?

'The "Symphony of Lights" is aptly named.' Marissa breathed the words and felt her senses come alive from all directions.

They were aboard an authentic junk on Victoria Harbour. Mr Qi had explained the meaning behind the themes but she'd got stuck on 'awakening' for she feared she had awakened to Rick and she didn't know what to do about it.

Rick stood behind her on the deck of the junk. To their left, bright orange sails caught the sea breeze with startling efficiency as they moved through the water. Rick's legs were braced. His hands held her lightly under her elbows and, if she leaned back just a little, she could pretend he held her as a lover would.

The war of emotion and delight and wonder and sensation battered at her from without and within, snatched her breath. All because of a powerful man in a business city that provided the perfect backdrop for all the things about him she had sworn she would never like, and now found she…liked too much.

A fringed end of brown silk shawl brushed

over her wrist and she stroked her fingers over the delicate fabric. 'You shouldn't have bought me this.' But she was glad he had. Her delight when she'd stepped into her room and found it on the bed had rippled through her.

She wore the jewelled band in her hair as well, felt rather like a princess in all her finery.

'The shawl matches the colour of your eyes. I couldn't resist it.' Maybe he didn't intend her to hear the low words, but she did, and she shivered in his hold.

After the light show they returned to land and ate in a traditional restaurant overlooking the harbour. Rick looked stunning in a dark suit and starched white shirt, the gold and onyx cuff-links at his wrists flashing occasionally when he gestured with the hands that had cupped her elbows with warmth and sweet tenderness during the light show.

His tie was burgundy silk. She'd bought it and had pushed it into his hands at the end of their shopping trip, and she liked to see it on him. Felt far too possessive about him.

Now, his gaze strayed to her continuously and his fingers idly stroked that tie as he talked business with their hosts until Marissa struggled to breathe normally, her heart and body awash with longing for him.

She'd fallen in love. She finally let the truth of it rise from deep in her heart, as soft as the whisper of silk against her skin, as frightening and devastating as the meaning of life.

Mr Qi had talked about the themes behind the light show while blue and red and green and yellow and pink light reflected off the water. Marissa had taken in the show but it was Rick's nearness at her back that had made her feel awakened. Now she longed for partnership and celebration with Rick but he didn't want that. He didn't want any of that with her.

She swallowed back the emotion that clogged her throat and dropped her gaze lest Rick see what was in her eyes.

'Thank you for organising for us to see the light show and for this wonderful evening.' Marissa addressed her words to Mr Qi, to all their hosts, tried to smile and seem natural as she praised the city, its beauty, the temples and age-old religions and staggering strength of the Hong Kong business world.

'We are pleased you've enjoyed our city.' Mr Qi turned to Rick. 'And pleased to create a business bond with Morgan's for our Australian building investments.' In his flawless English Mr Qi went on to outline the group's decision.

Rick murmured words of appreciation.

Two more hours passed before they finally wrapped up the evening. By then every nerve in Marissa's body was stretched tight. She hadn't set out to love Rick—couldn't believe she'd allowed it to happen—but she did and she didn't know what to do about it. She wanted a family with him. Wanted *his* babies. Wanted him to tell her that thirty wasn't so old and that he thought she was beautiful and always would think that, even when she was very old indeed...

When they got back to Australia she'd return to Gordon's office. Would Rick remember her? Think about her? Or quickly forget her and go back to a brief nod as he swept by, his thoughts centred on his work and not the woman who had helped him with it for a short time?

They left with handshakes and bows and the assurance of a deal large enough and lucrative enough to raise Rick's business profile more than ever. At the last moment Mr Qi presented

Rick with an embossed envelope. 'Perhaps you might like these.'

Rick thanked him, tucked the envelope inside his inner jacket pocket and then they were away. He took her back across the harbour. It was like crossing a big river and, before she was ready for it, they were inside their Kowloon hotel once again.

Rick took Marissa to her room in silence, so attracted to her in the lovely dress and all the more to the softness in her eyes and the guarded vulnerability there. He held her shawl. It had slipped from her shoulders as they'd crossed the harbour and he'd taken it into his hands, the soft fabric warmed from her body.

She paused outside her room. Turned to face him. 'Thank you for a wonderful day, for the gifts.' Her hand rose to touch the jewelled band that held her curls off her face.

His hand lifted to her shoulder, captured a lock of her hair and pressed it between thumb and finger, because he couldn't stand not touching her, yet it only made him want her more. 'I'm glad you wore your hair down tonight. It's you. So vital and alive and free.'

If she knew how much he wanted to bury his

face in that mass of curls, to inhale the essence of her and hold her and somehow wrap her around him and inside him…

'I don't ever look sleek and neat as a pin, no matter how hard I try.' Her lips tilted in a soft attempt at a smile.

'You look…' Holdable. Kissable. 'It's you. I hope you never change.'

'It won't matter. Soon you won't even notice me. You'll go back to passing me in the corridors with a nod—'

'No.' He didn't know if he could ever dismiss her from his thoughts. Rick tugged her into his arms before he knew his own intention, took the possibility of other words from her mouth with his lips.

As his arms closed about her and her mouth warmed beneath his, he fought his demons and didn't know any more whether he had lost or won, only that he needed her.

How could holding her be such torment? How could he let her go?

She drew back with a gasp. A pulse fluttered at the base of her throat. Her eyes were wide and uncertain, filled with desire and…anguish.

'Marissa—'

'Wh-what did Mr Qi give you before we left?' Her words were an attempt to draw back from the brink.

He blinked and struggled with harsh stark feelings that tore at him. Why had he thought he could bring her here and not want to make love with her? That he could give her the sights and sounds of Hong Kong and not want her for himself?

He tugged the envelope from his pocket and flipped it open. There were photos. Two of them, taken at the petting zoo. Mr Qi had had the digital images made into prints for them. In the first photo Marissa had the koala in her arms. She smiled and, behind her, Rick smiled for the cameras. He stared unblinkingly at that first photo for a moment before he tilted it forward.

The one behind it made him catch his breath because in this photo her heart was in her eyes. The wounds she'd sustained when her fiancé had dumped her, her need to know she could connect in a meaningful way again and have it work out for her. The ache in her as she'd held that bundle of fur in her arms. Her tender feelings for the man in the picture.

He was that man, and he wanted those feelings

from her even as he recognised the expression in his eyes in the picture. Longing, hunger. He'd thought it wouldn't show. Hadn't realised the strength of those feelings, even then. The thought of making love to her, of giving her something she wanted and thus locking her irrevocably to him in the process, rushed him, shocked him. Even as he admitted he'd known all along that longing for a child had been part of her reaction that day.

'A couple of prints from the petting zoo.' He cleared his throat, turned the envelope so she could see the top print, and then tucked the small packet back into his pocket.

His desire to kiss her, possess her, tore at him and he backed away from it and from her because if he touched her at all he wouldn't stop. 'It's late and we have a long flight ahead of us to get home tomorrow.'

'To get back to work and our usual tasks. In my case, anyway. You'll just go on as before, but with Tom.' Marissa almost asked Rick to stay. The words trembled on the tip of her tongue but, before she could find the courage to say them, or the sanity to stop herself, he took the decision from her.

'Goodnight.' There was a bite in his voice that

was self-derision and intensity and longing and refusal wrapped into one. His room was across from hers. He entered and closed the door with a soft click that seemed far too final.

She sagged for a harsh, struggling moment before she let herself into her own room, and with a sound wrenched from her, fell back against the door. Her spine welcomed the hard surface, the chill inanimateness of it, while her heart railed at her, told her to go to him—

She tugged the jewelled decoration from her hair, set is on the bedside table. Thought of Rick in that room across the hall, so close. Took a stumbling step towards the door.

The rap from the other side made her heart slam in her chest. She lunged for the doorknob and wrenched the door open and knew, *knew in her heart that if there was any way she could keep him with her, even just for the one night, she would*. All thoughts of self-preservation were gone, lost to her, because if she could only love him once then she wanted to.

He held her shawl crushed inside a white-knuckled fist. He didn't even pretend it was the reason. 'Tell me no, Marissa. Tell it to me right now.'

She drew a shaken breath. Her fingers wrapped around his strong hair-roughened wrist. 'I need you tonight, Rick. Here and now. I'm only prepared to tell you that.'

CHAPTER FOURTEEN

RICK crossed the threshold of Marissa's room without any awareness that he had moved. He only felt her body in his arms as the door clicked locked behind him and his mouth came down over hers.

It wasn't an easy kiss, or a soft one. He covered her lips with his and took every part of her that she would give. Possessed and suckled and stroked until his blood bubbled in his veins and his body shook and his emotions roiled and he didn't know how to quiet them, how to assuage them.

'I want this.' She sighed the words into the crook of his neck and pressed her lips to his skin there.

He buried his free hand in her hair, lodged it deep in the wild curliness as he tipped up her head to give him the access he wanted to her mouth. Her chin and face and neck.

The need for her turned molten, raged through him and made his knees quake and his heart stutter with—

Not longing. Not a need so deep it was unfathomable. He could not acknowledge that, be at the mercy of that. Yet his hand in her hair gentled to reverent pressure as he brought her head forward and let himself have the softness of her, the sweetness of her as their lips touched, brushed, in the gentle kiss he should have given her to start with.

He tossed the shawl onto the bed behind them, a splash of brown against the soft golden tone of the quilt.

Let him please her, wring everything from this time with her—for both of them. Let him at least have that, give her that. It was a supplication and a hope and a determination as Rick gave himself—all of him that he could—to the woman in his arms.

Stroking hands over her hair and the skin of her arms. Whisper-soft kisses to soothe the startled sensitivity of her lips where he had kissed her.

Where Marissa had ached from Rick's focused plundering of her senses, her heart melted in the face of his gentleness. The man, the layers, the complexities. Maybe no person would ever truly know all of him and, despite the ache in her heart for him and for the knowledge that he didn't share her feelings, he felt something.

He gave her something. Perhaps more of himself than Michael had ever given.

The thought surfaced and she pushed it away because Michael was a shadow. A piece of the past.

Rick was real and here in her arms and if her heart broke tomorrow and went on breaking she would have to find a way to survive it somehow because she couldn't end this. She would not deny herself this.

So she would give him her heart in her touch and the haven of her arms, just this one time. It was madness and insanity and the essence of a need so deep she couldn't fathom it. She faced it and chose it.

'I want to feel your warmth.' She needed that.

Her hands pushed his jacket off broad shoulders, down muscular arms, flung it across the chair behind him. With shaking fingertips she traced the hard heat of his chest, touched the silk tie.

'I'm glad you wore this.' The sight of it on him had raised proprietorial instincts she hadn't known she had.

The primitive emotions warned her how far she had fallen. She didn't want to know. Not now. Not yet.

'I'm glad you wore the dress and shawl.' His words were a low growl as her fingers worked the tie out from beneath his collar.

His hands roved restlessly up and down her arms. She sensed both urgency and his restraint, the war of the two inside him. The tie disappeared and the flat of his hand pressed into her back between her shoulders, pressed her forward until their bodies locked once more.

'You bought them for me.' Clothes he had wanted her to have. Clothes she had wanted to wear for him.

'And you put them on with those dainty high heeled shoes and all I could think about all night was touching you, your beautiful legs wrapping around me, welcoming me.' He made a harsh sound and stroked his thumbs over the points of her jaw. 'Since that day when I lifted you into my car I've thought about your legs—'

He kissed her and praised her and murmured all the ways he wanted to show her how beautiful he thought her, and Marissa forgot about coffee table analogies and fear and what would happen tomorrow, and lost herself in him.

Rick's hands shifted to the back of her dress and his gaze was intent on hers as he set her skin free inch by inch until cool air touched her back and warm fingers skimmed over her spine.

This was really happening and she made the choice to take everything, give everything that could be shared, to awaken and celebrate in this moment, with him.

'I need your hands on me.' He lifted her hand to his mouth, kissed her fingers and placed them against his chest over the fabric of his shirt. 'On my skin. Over my heart. Please, Marissa.'

The gravelly plea curled around her heart. He must feel something for her. His rough plea suggested he did, his gaze echoed it. Need. He did need her somehow.

She stepped back and his arms dropped to his sides. Spiky lashes swept down as his gaze locked on her mouth, roved her body with possessive intent and with awe.

She released the buttons on his shirt one by one. Feasted with her fingertips upon the skin stretched tight across his muscled chest, let the abrasion of dark curly hair fill her senses. One cuff-link came away. The other. He shrugged the shirt off his shoulders and flung it away, wrapped her in arms that felt as though they could shelter her for ever.

Then Marissa's breath caught on a stifled sound of longing that came not only from her senses but also from deep in her soul and heart.

He tipped up her chin and searched her eyes and emotions warred in his gaze before he crushed her close, his hands flat against her back as he pushed clothing away. 'Say my name. I need to hear it.'

'Only you, Rick.' She had no room in her heart or her senses for any other. 'I only want to think of you, of this—this moment.'

His arms trembled as he laid her on the bed. He reached into the pocket of his trousers, laid a small foil packet on the night-stand beside her and bowed his head as though fighting with himself somehow.

Marissa let her gaze encompass that gesture and swallowed hard. 'I thought you might have to raid the supplies in the bathroom.'

She could tell him she was on the pill, that she'd stayed on it since Michael, but she didn't want to bring the other man's name into the room. It would feel like sacrilege.

Rick knelt on the floor at her side, stroked skin too tight and too hot and stripped away the layers until she was naked before him—and naked emotionally—and she shuddered with vulnerable need and would have covered herself.

'Don't.' He spoke that single hoarse word and his arms closed around her. He buried his face against her heart and shuddered, a strong man on his knees and emotionally vulnerable to her. Right now, that was who he was, as vulnerable as her.

She clasped his shoulders and tugged. 'Come to me. Please, Rick.'

Rick shed the rest of his clothes and joined Marissa, drew her into the hold of his arms and against his body, and they touched in so many places finally.

He was drowning in Marissa's arms, in an overload of wrenching feeling that welled up from somewhere deep inside. His hands shook as he ran them over her face, caressed her neck and shoulders and the dip of her waist.

A convulsive swallow made him aware of the tightness in his throat as he buried his gaze in soft brown eyes blurred with warmth and longing.

'This night.' He spoke the words, a benediction and a warning and a promise. 'For this night you're mine.'

'And you're mine.' Her arms bound him to her. 'For tonight *you're mine.*'

He hadn't known anything of pleasure. Not until now and it swamped his senses, poured over him and through him and her fierce words were right at the centre of it.

When she opened herself to him, his heart filled with aching wonder and stark desperation. He loved her with his body and his touch and his senses, with everything within him he still didn't fully understand and when it ended, he kissed her and, cradled her in his arms and didn't want to leave her.

Eventually he forced himself to release her. He padded to the bathroom, and returned to her side and climbed back into the bed. His arms tightened around her and he couldn't prevent the tight sigh of sound that escaped as he buried his face in her hair.

He didn't know how to handle the overload of feeling, the possessiveness that rose up, the wild thoughts of finding ways to make Marissa stay with him, to keep her at his side. The temptation to take her again without benefit of any package…

'You were all I needed,' she whispered as she

drifted into sleep. 'In the end, you were all of it anyway. I hadn't realised…'

And she'd been all to him, despite those temptations. He held her until she slept and he stayed at her side, his arms around her, and felt the hours slide away one after another until there were too many gone and he felt panicky and lost and somehow shattered because she *had* been all, but she was wrong that he'd been enough for her.

He rose from the bed then, quietly retrieved and donned his clothes.

Brushed his fingers over the shawl abandoned at the foot of the bed and took the memory of her hair spread across the pillow, her soft mouth and the touch and taste of her with him as he left the room.

As he backed away emotionally, just as his father had done for as long as Rick could remember. Wasn't that what he was doing?

You don't want to hurt her. The way your father has hurt Kirri and your sisters and would have hurt your mother if she didn't choose to push it all away.

It was sound reasoning.

Why did it leave him so hollow inside?

* * *

To: Sanfrandani, Englishcrumpet
From Kangagirl
So much has happened in such a short space of time, I don't know where to start. Well, I guess it doesn't matter where I start. The ending is still the same. I fell in love with Rick and he doesn't feel the same way but I don't want you to worry about me because I'll get over it. Tomorrow when I go to work I'll be back in Gordon's office.

Rick's secretary will be back, you see, so he won't need me any more, and my boss will be back, so it all works out. I'm glad, really. And it's my birthday on Friday. I've entertained a lot of nonsense thoughts about turning thirty. As though the day means anything, really.

And I bought you both a little something in Hong Kong. You can expect a small package each in the mail in the next week or two, depending on the vagaries of the postal service at either end...

To: Englishcrumpet
From: Sanfrandani
I'm worried about Marissa. She's so generous, thinking about us when it's clear her heart is breaking. I don't know how to help her. I wish she hadn't fallen for this guy. That's twice in a row that she's loved and ended up devastated, and this time it seems even worse for her. It doesn't seem fair!

To: Sanfrandani
From: Englishcrumpet
All we can do is be there for her. I wonder if she could have avoided this? Love seems to survive even the greatest resistance sometimes, whether it's welcome or not.

CHAPTER FIFTEEN

'MARISSA. I didn't expect to see you here.'

The male voice was familiar. Marissa looked up into Michael Unsworth's bland, suave face and blinked her eyes. He had to be a mirage. Fate wouldn't be so cruel as to do this to her just days short of her birthday, when she already felt miserable and depressed and…heartbroken for a man who simply didn't want to love her or even keep her in his life. Not his personal life, not his close working life.

Rick Morgan was that man. Not this echo of the past.

But here Michael stood, right in the middle of the coffee shop she'd slipped away to for lunch. 'Michael. Excuse me. I'm late getting back to work.'

It was only the barest of white lies. She looked at the man and she felt nothing but a distanced dislike because of his shabby past behaviour.

Rick had her heart. There was no room for any other. Not in any way.

'Er…look, Marissa, I didn't intend for you to find out this way.' Michael's voice oozed sympathy but the feeling didn't reach his eyes. 'Especially so close to your…er…well…to your birthday. I promise you if I'd known you'd be anywhere near this place—'

'I can't imagine why you would be concerned about seeing me near my birthday or any other time, and the last time I checked, people could eat where they liked.' Marissa didn't want to revisit his earlier birthday promise to her—that they would be secretly engaged and eventually get married and love each other for ever.

How could she have been so foolish as to even think she'd fallen for him anyway? He wasn't half the man Rick was.

And how could you be so foolish as to love Rick, who told you he would never commit to you?

'Who is this, Michael? A friend of yours?' A woman drew level with them.

Several things registered with Marissa in that moment. The woman was Jane McCullough, the daughter of Michael's company boss. The two of them were clearly together. And Jane was pregnant.

The feelings Marissa had thought she had under control about having a child made themselves known again then. 'You... You're expecting a baby.' Her voice wobbled. 'Congratulations.'

And Jane was much younger than thirty. Probably no more than twenty-five...

'Marissa, this is my fiancée, Jane McCullough.' Michael inserted the words with a hint of warning in his tone.

What did he think she would do? Tear out the other woman's eyes because she had him and Marissa didn't, because she was starting the family Marissa now knew she would never, ever have? If she couldn't have that with Rick, she would never want it with anyone.

'We've met in passing, though I don't know if Jane would remember her father introducing us.' Marissa offered a polite nod to the woman. A smile was beyond her right now. 'I hope you're keeping well.'

I hope Michael is true to you, truer than he ever was to me.

Jane frowned as she apparently considered the significance of Marissa's past involvement with Michael.

And Marissa excused herself a second time and walked away. The only good thing she could think of as she stepped back into the Morgan company building was that at least she'd eaten a wholesome sandwich and even a piece of fruit for her lunch. 'There'll be no fainting on the job today.'

Rick would be proud, but it wasn't about Rick any more. Hadn't been since they'd got off the plane days ago and he'd finally faced her fully.

'If the protection fails and there's a baby, I'll take care of you. I expect you to let me know.'

That was what he had said, the only words about the night they'd shared, the most wonderful experience of her life and she'd thought it had meant something special to him as well. In her heart she still believed it had, but just not enough. He'd looked at her then with such anguish in his eyes, but ultimately he'd turned away.

They'd spoken since. Awkward words when she'd bumped into him on her floor, when he'd dropped by Gordon's office to speak to him, and twice when Rick had visited the company's cafeteria at the same time she had.

She didn't remember seeing that much of him before she'd started working for him. Maybe he'd been there but she hadn't truly noticed. Now she noticed everything, longed for each glimpse of him. How could she go on day after day this way? Seeing him, speaking briefly with him while their gazes locked and she fought all her longing for him and needed him so much she kept thinking she saw the same longing in him?

It had to end. The torture had to end but she didn't know how to make that happen.

'Marissa.' Rick stepped into the lift behind the woman he couldn't get out of his mind. 'I thought I might see you at the cafeteria today.' He'd been looking, going places she might be…

'I went out instead.' Her low words were guarded.

He stood beside her and felt helpless. And then she raised her hand to press the button for her floor, as she had done that very first day, and all the moments they had shared since then washed through him and he realised…

He'd fallen in love with her. The ache in his chest couldn't be anything else. The need to be near her any way he could…

'You…er…where are you going? You haven't pressed for a floor.' Her mouth softened to a vulnerable line as she looked at him for one brief moment, seemed to take in every feature as though she needed to commit him to her memory as much as he needed to be with her.

I'm going to whatever floor keeps me with you in here the longest.

'Er…the top floor. Swimming.' In truth, he hadn't been up there for ages. He'd lost interest in most of the things he routinely did, had only kept going with his work because it made the time pass. *He loved her.* Where did he go with that? He, who hadn't believed he could…

Marissa pressed the button for the top floor and the floor she shared with Gordon, and her hand dropped to her side. He wanted to capture her fingers in his and never let go. He wanted a chance with her. His heart leaped into his throat and stayed there. Words pushed past anyway. 'Please, will you—'

Ding.

The lift stopped, the doors slid open. She glanced at him and a choked sound came from her throat. 'I have to go. I have to get back to work. I can't—' She stepped out of the lift and was gone.

But maybe not completely gone from him? As the lift doors closed and he felt as though his heart had stayed behind on that other floor with her, Rick pondered that emotional leap.

He wasn't like his father. How could he be when this love in his chest, this need for Marissa, filled all of him? He just hadn't known what love was—the real, strong, all-encompassing love of a man for only one woman.

Was it too late? He didn't know, but he understood now what he had to do…

Her birthday was almost over. Well, the working part of it was over at least. For the first time, Marissa had contemplated calling in and pretending she was sick so she wouldn't have to go to work today.

But she'd gone to work and she'd got through the day without even a glimpse of the company boss, and now all she had to do was manage the birthday dinner her parents had sprung on her after all.

Marissa left her apartment and climbed into the taxi her mother had arranged for her. She even managed a slight smile as she thought how much Mum must have enjoyed putting together this 'little surprise', complete with an 'undisclosed destination' for this taxi ride.

Hopefully the driver knew where he was taking her!

Well, Marissa would enjoy the night if it killed her. She owed her parents that much.

Eighty-eight storeys above ground level, Rick waited in a restaurant in Sydney's Centrepoint Tower building. The tables faced panels of glass that gave a moving panoramic view of the harbour and city.

Rick only had eyes for the woman who followed the waitress towards the table set for eight. Marissa wore the silk dress bought in Hong Kong, the shawl spread across her shoulders. Her face held determination and unhappiness she was working very hard to mask, and surprise. That last was the result of believing her parents had sprung a birthday event on her after all, no doubt, and of that 'surprise' leading her here.

He'd begged for her parents' co-operation to make tonight happen, had laid himself bare to get it, and after a thorough grilling from Abe and a gentler one from Tilda, they'd come through for him. Tilda had admitted that Marissa had made it clear she didn't want to celebrate this birthday, that the date itself had unpleasant memories for her, thanks to her ex-fiancé, and, on top of that, her daughter didn't seem to be coping very well with the idea of turning thirty.

To Rick, Marissa's age was perfect. *She* was perfect. He'd chosen this restaurant because he wanted to lay all of the city at her feet. Maybe that was whimsical, but he'd gone with his heart. Now he had to convince Marissa of his love, and convince her to let him love her and prove those thoughts to her. If she would let him. If she could find something in her heart for him.

Would her smile fade and utter rejection replace it when she noticed him? Had he left it too late and lost her, if he ever truly had a chance with her in the first place? His fingers moved to the outline of the ring in his pocket and for a long moment his breath froze in his chest and he thought his lungs might give out and he'd end up on the floor.

He knew the precise moment she spotted him, noted his presence, instead of her parents.

In fact, Abe and Tilda were here, waiting beyond them tucked away near the bar with Rick's sisters and nieces. Close enough to know the significance of this meeting, far enough away not to overhear any softly spoken words and not to distract Marissa during these first moments.

Marissa's step hitched. Unease bloomed in her too-pale face. Her gaze shifted to the empty seats at the table and came back to him, and she started to turn away.

'Please don't leave without hearing me out. When you've done that, if need be, I'll be the one to go.' His heart hammered as he stepped forward.

'I don't understand. I was supposed to meet Mum and Dad. How… Why…?'

'I asked them to help me arrange this. I phoned your father and talked him into this because I realized…I had to do this…' There were no smooth words and his throat tightened and an inexplicable rush of emotion swamped him.

'You're so beautiful tonight.' So beautiful it squeezed his heart just to look at her. 'I'll always remember how you looked in that dress the first night you wore it.' And afterwards, as he'd stripped it away from her and they'd joined in the most intimate way possible.

Why hadn't he realised then that he loved her?

That his *heart* needed her? Why hadn't he come home to her then?

'I want you to go. My parents must be on their way and I don't want them to know how I feel…' She stopped the words.

They stood beside the end of the table, and instinctively he caught her hands in his. There were diners all around them, people enjoying the wonder and pleasure of the night as though dining in the sky itself.

He could only see the woman before him and he spoke in a low tone filled with the emotion inside him because he couldn't hold back the words. He didn't want to. She had to have all of them, all of this, he'd finally realised. 'I thought if I stayed away from you that would be best for you.'

To tell her with her parents and his sisters waiting was the only way he could think of to let her know he meant this. That he would risk everything.

Rick took a deep breath. 'I told myself you would find someone better, someone who didn't have the issues behind him that I do. But I love you, Marissa, with all my heart and mind and soul. I didn't understand what it meant when I made love with you that night and didn't ever want to let you go, but I know now.'

A soft sound came from her throat and she swallowed hard. 'Don't do this to me, Rick. Don't say things like this to me when you can't mean them.'

'I mean them. I mean all of it.' He drew her forward. His arms ached to hold her and for a moment the ruthless side of his nature goaded him to simply pull her into his embrace and try to get what he wanted through a connection they had already proved, but he wouldn't do that.

Because she deserved all of it, even if at the end she turned him away.

'You made it clear you wouldn't love me, that you only wanted that one night. That you wanted to be single. Because of your family history.' Marissa didn't know what to do. She wanted to turn away, to rush out of this glittery setting that spread all of Sydney at her feet but, with Rick's hands on hers, she couldn't move at all.

She couldn't make herself break even this tenuous hold, and she couldn't stop the hope that rose in her heart. 'You don't have to feel sorry for me or think because I'm turning thirt—'

'I'm seven years older, Marissa. You might

consider that too old, I don't know. I don't care about either of our ages because I only want you, and I swear I'll make you forget your ex-fiancé.' His words were tortured but determined. 'If you'll just give me the chance, say you'll stay with me, maybe one day you'll learn to love me, to want me.

'I know what I told you, that I couldn't commit. You understood why I believed that, but I was wrong. I know this because you have all my heart. Every part of it.'

It was the most humbling and loving of speeches and her hands squeezed his as she felt the eyes of people around on them, but she could only see Rick, only look into deep grey eyes that couldn't seem to shift their gaze from her.

'If you're worried I'll be pregnant, I'm sure I won't be. You took care of me.'

Could Rick truly love her? Oh, Marissa wanted to believe it, but how could it be true?

'It's not about a possible pregnancy, though I want my baby growing inside you.' He uttered the words in a low tone filled with need. 'I want lots of babies with you, as many as will make you happy and I want them for myself too. I want you working at my side or at least close by every day and I want us to go home to the same bed at night. Most of all, I just want the chance to love you.'

'Oh, Rick. I want those things with you.' They would be a dream come true, better than any plan she could have conjured up and tried to set into motion through Blinddatebrides.com. He didn't know about that, about exactly how she'd gone about her dating efforts.

'I don't want to hold back any more. Not from you. Not ever from you.' His hand rose to cup her face, to skim over her hair, as he seemed to search for words. Finally he spoke them, his gaze never wavering from hers. 'I've spent a lifetime pushing down the fact that my family isn't perfect, that my father couldn't meet certain emotional needs. I thought I couldn't do any better.

'What I didn't realise is I *did* fill the gaps he left. Darla helped me see that, and I don't have to feel guilty for acknowledging how he is.'

Marissa's heart ached for him. 'No. You're not to blame for any of that.'

'I want to follow the example of *your* father, and love with all my heart. I want to love *you* that way, Marissa, if you'll let me.' His gaze seemed to worship every part of her as his hands rose to stroke her arms, to gently cup them in strong palms. 'Years ago I thought I was in love, but the feelings… weren't real. Not like what I feel for you. I backed away, and I thought I did it because I was like my father, but I know now that wasn't it. I didn't love her because she wasn't you, because I could only love you. I was waiting for you.'

His mouth softened and his eyes softened and all his love for her welled into the air between them until she had to believe it, couldn't deny it any longer.

'Oh, Rick.' Marissa's breath caught. She clasped his arms where he held her, wrapped her hands around thick muscle covered in the constraint of cloth and remembered those strong arms holding her as he'd gently led her to paradise. 'You truly love me?'

'Yes.' His voice dropped to a low whisper. 'Yes, if you'll let me, I will love you for the rest of my life and I swear I'll never let you down or leave you wondering or wishing I'd given you more, opened to you more. You'll have all of me, Marissa, the good and the bad, if you'll take me.'

The sounds around them seemed to fade to nothing as she stared into his eyes. Outside, the city lights winked and seemed to tell her the time had come. That this *was* the real thing and somehow, magically, it had come to her, despite her fears and her foolish worry about getting older and her joining a dating site so she could hand pick her fate, as though that were possible.

'I want to agree,' she whispered and his hands tightened and his muscles seemed to lock as he stood before her, waiting. 'But there are things you don't know about me. About what I've been doing, what I've wanted out of life and how I went about trying to get those things.'

'Like looking on a dating website?' He didn't seem the least surprised, or concerned. 'That day you fell asleep in your apartment and I fell asleep on your sofa, I came into your room and saw the site on your laptop. When I realised how much I love you I thought about joining up and trying to woo you from there, but I didn't want to wait that long to tell you how I felt. Once I realised how much I love you—'

'I was going to hand pick a man exactly right for me.' The words burst out of her—a confession, an admission of the ignorance of her plans. 'I thought if I made my choice clinically I'd be able to guard myself, not get hurt.'

His fingers stroked up and down her arms while his gaze lingered on each feature of her face and finally came back to look deep into her eyes. 'I'm not perfect. I'm far from it, but I love you with all my heart and I'm hoping that will count for something. And I won't put my career before you. I want you to know that because I think your ex-fiancé did that.' He made it a vow as his hands lifted until his fingers were in her hair. 'I'll make whatever changes are needed so that can never happen because you will always be first with me. Over and above everything.'

How her heart soared then and, even as it did, she knew she had to be equally honest. 'It was foolish of me to believe I could find love the way I planned to.

'I looked at the pictures of happy couples and I wanted that too because I'd been used and humiliated. I thought my heart had been broken but I didn't love him. Not the way I love you. I could never love anyone the way I love you and I realise now that you can't choose love. It comes to you. It finds you.'

'It found me the day I looked at a woman with a hard hat squashed down over her curls and a sparkle in her eyes.' He drew her hand to his chest, pressed it over his heart where she could absorb the deep beat.

A beat that told her how much he meant this. 'It stuck around as she called the photocopier names and rushed to be at her mother's side and lay in my arms in a bed in a borrowed garage and a bed in a sumptuous hotel room on the other side of the world. I bought the clothes because I didn't want you to forget me, but I can't forget you.'

He clasped her hands in his and there, in front of the entire restaurant, he drew something bright and glittery from his pocket, held it between his fingertips and went down on one knee. 'Please say you'll marry me, Marissa. Give us a chance. Let me give you all the things you've been longing for.'

'I want to marry you, spend my life with you.' Her heart hitched as his fingers tightened over hers, and one final confession poured out of her. 'I bought baby wool. To knit booties. I really do want a baby and I don't think that's something that's going to go away. But I want a baby…with you, not with anyone else.'

His fingers wrapped so hard around hers, he

almost crushed them. 'That's…I want that more than I can tell you.'

'Oh, Rick.' And she let go of the last foolish fear, the pride that had led her to try to find Mr Right in all the wrong ways when he had been there in front of her all the time. 'I love you with all my heart.' The words came *straight from* her heart.

His fingers trembled as he wrapped them around hers. The mouth that was usually firm and commanding wobbled a little too as he held the ring at the tip of her finger and looked into her eyes as though seeking her permission. She swallowed hard and, through a sheen of tears, looked at the exquisite ring.

'I asked Mr Qi to get it for me.' Rick cleared his throat. 'Actually, I talked him into flying it out here personally with a whole bunch of paperwork from the jeweller's and other stuff to make sure it could be delivered straight to me. I spotted it that day we were there…'

He'd gone to all this trouble for her. To make this special for her. A birthday to remember, so different from that other one. Her voice was a whisper of love and need as she said finally, 'Then I think I'd like to wear it now, if you truly do want this.'

'I do.' He slid the ring home, a perfect fit and the perfect symbol of all he felt for her.

And then, as she tugged on his hand, he got to his feet and crushed her into his arms and she felt his deep shudder of relief and longing as he pressed his face into her neck and murmured her name over and over.

'Thank you, my darling.' His fingers found their way through her hair to her nape. 'Thank you for putting your trust in me.'

'I love you, Rick.' Her hands touched his arms, his shoulders. 'I love you so much.'

He kissed her then, in front of the diners and the waiters and all of Sydney outside the sparkling windows.

When they finally broke apart, pleased laughter and murmurs of 'Hear, hear!' and 'How lovely!' broke out around them.

Rick drew Marissa around then, and she gasped.

Mum and Dad, Darla and Faith and Kirrilea and little Julia all stood there. They smiled, grinned. Her Mum and Darla and Faith had tears in their eyes.

Marissa's gaze flew to Rick's. 'You asked me in front of all of them. You went down on your knees in front of not only the strangers in this room, but in front of your family and mine. If I'd said no—'

'I wanted you to have your proposal in front of everyone so you'd know I meant it, that I would put my heart on the line for you.' A wealth of determination and love and understanding and hope shone in his eyes. 'Especially in front of the people that matter the most to both of us.'

His parents weren't among that number. Had he asked them to come, only to have them turn him down?

'It doesn't matter, Marissa.' He seemed to read her thoughts. *'You're here.'*

'And *most* of our family are here.' His and hers—and they would share that family.

Marissa promised herself there and then that she would weave Rick into *her* family, with Mum and Dad and Aunty Jean and the others, and she would work equally as hard to be part of his family, with his sisters and his nieces and, yes, his parents, who cared to a degree but also had their faults.

She wrapped her arms around his shoulders and drew his head down and kissed him fiercely, and when they broke apart and he told her she certainly knew how to pick her moments, she laughed and linked their arms together.

'I'm picking *every moment* for us, from now until forever.' And Marissa raised her voice and told the man she loved, 'Because you're my Mr Absolutely Right and you always will be, and I want the world to know I love you exactly as you are. I don't want *you* to change in any way.'

There were hugs all around and eventually they sat down to dine and celebrate a birthday that had turned out to be a milestone for a very different reason.

Marissa looked at Rick's ring on her finger and thought of being with him, of going home with him day after day. Old? One day she hoped to be. With Rick, and their children around them.

As their family spoke among themselves and the meals were brought out, Rick touched the shawl at her shoulders and bent his dark head to hers. 'I'm going to marry you with a big wedding and all the trimmings and all of Sydney looking on. I hope you're ready for that.'

'Maybe not *all* of Sydney. That would be rather a crowd.' But her smile broke through. 'I do want the world to know I'm yours, and you're mine, and I'd like to share our joy with as many people as we can.' She fell silent. 'A big wedding would take a lot of planning, though, and it would mean we'd have to wait months for it.'

'I'll put a team onto the matter. One of those wedding planner teams.' It was his turn to fall silent, but not for long. 'Everything has to be perfect for you but if I keep a close enough eye on it all…'

A glint of corporate determination filled his gaze.

She watched the plans click over and his expression become more and more focused and her heart melted for him all over again.

'You'll move in with me before then, won't you? Now that I have you, I don't want to let you go.' He hesitated. 'Or I can move in with you. Anywhere you want; I just want us to be together. I want to wake up every day with you at my side, make love to you until I've shown you how much I love you, how much you mean to me.'

A lifetime of togetherness. Her heart filled and she twined her fingers with his, simply because she could. 'Then I think maybe we should start on that plan as soon as possible and I would like to live in your apartment, at least at first. Later we might want a…different location.'

'For our children.' The possessive words wrapped her in desire and warmth and promise. 'For when *our* family of two becomes three or more.' He lowered his voice again. 'I want to make love to you quite desperately right now, Marissa Warren.'

The first opportunity they got, after the cake and the good wishes, they slipped away.

And later, as Marissa lay in Rick's arms and he told her again how much he loved her, she gasped.

He rose up on one elbow and looked into her eyes. 'What is it?'

'I've just realised I have a little explaining to do to my Blinddatebrides.com friends. At least my subscription has a few months left to run, so I can keep using the IM facility to chat with them, and I can check out profiles for them.'

Rick barely flinched before he relaxed again. 'I'll help you, if you like. Just so long as you take *your* profile off the "available" listings.'

'The only man I want to be available to is you.' She kissed him and they lost themselves again.

And, a very long time later, Marissa murmured, 'I wonder which of my online friends—Dani or Grace—will be next to find *her* Mr Right on Blinddatebrides.com?'

MILLS & BOON PUBLISH EIGHT LARGE PRINT TITLES A MONTH. THESE ARE THE EIGHT TITLES FOR AUGUST 2009.

THE SPANISH BILLIONAIRE'S PREGNANT WIFE
Lynne Graham

THE ITALIAN'S RUTHLESS MARRIAGE COMMAND
Helen Bianchin

THE BRUNELLI BABY BARGAIN
Kim Lawrence

THE FRENCH TYCOON'S PREGNANT MISTRESS
Abby Green

DIAMOND IN THE ROUGH
Diana Palmer

SECRET BABY, SURPRISE PARENTS
Liz Fielding

THE REBEL KING
Melissa James

NINE-TO-FIVE BRIDE
Jennie Adams

MILLS & BOON

MILLS & BOON PUBLISH EIGHT LARGE PRINT TITLES A MONTH. THESE ARE THE EIGHT TITLES FOR SEPTEMBER 2009.

***

THE SICILIAN BOSS'S MISTRESS
Penny Jordan

PREGNANT WITH THE BILLIONAIRE'S BABY
Carole Mortimer

THE VENADICCI MARRIAGE VENGEANCE
Melanie Milburne

THE RUTHLESS BILLIONAIRE'S VIRGIN
Susan Stephens

ITALIAN TYCOON, SECRET SON
Lucy Gordon

ADOPTED: FAMILY IN A MILLION
Barbara McMahon

THE BILLIONAIRE'S BABY
Nicola Marsh

BLIND-DATE BABY
Fiona Harper